Because of the Rabbit

CYNTHIA LORD

Because of the Rabbit

Scholastic Press / New York

All rights reserved. Published by Scholastic Press, an imprint of Scholastic Inc., *Publishers since 1920.* SCHOLASTIC, SCHOLASTIC PRESS, and associated logos are trademarks and/or registered trademarks of Scholastic Inc.

The publisher does not have any control over and does not assume any responsibility for author or third-party websites or their content.

Library of Congress Cataloging-in-Publication Data available

ISBN 978-0-545-91424-6

10 9 8 7 6 5 4 3 2   20 21 22 23

Printed in the U.S.A.   23
First edition, April 2019
Book design by Nina Goffi

To Tami, who loves animals as much as I do

Rabbits are crepuscular, most active at dawn and dusk.

"A rabbit?" I heard Dad say into the phone. "Is he hurt?"

Mom sighed at the bowl of mashed potatoes in her hands. She likes it when all four of us can eat supper together, but when a Maine Game Warden gets a call, he has to go. Even if it's suppertime and tomorrow is the biggest day of my life.

"How long's the rabbit been there?" Dad asked.

Mom had made all my favorite foods—meat loaf, mashed potatoes, corn on the cob, and blueberry pie for dessert—but I was too excited to eat very much.

My older brother, Owen, leaned toward me. "Who's ahead? Excited or Scared?"

I grinned. When we were little, whenever we had mixed feelings about something, Owen and I'd pretend those feelings were running in a race. We hadn't done it in a long time, though.

"Excited is way ahead, but Scared is coming on strong," I said.

Mom passed me the bowl of mashed potatoes. "I'm sure most kids feel that way on the night before school starts."

I nodded, though we both knew I wasn't "most kids." Most kids went to school for the first time in preschool.

Or kindergarten.

Or maybe first grade.

Not many started in fifth. In fact, I was pretty sure I'd be the only fifth grader at Lakeview Elementary School who'd never gone off to school before.

It wasn't that I hadn't done school*work*. I'd done plenty. My lessons had been at the kitchen table, though. Science experiments were done in the bathroom or on the front porch—in case they exploded or leaked. I read books on my bed or on the couch or even floating in a kayak on the lake in front of our house.

Being homeschooled had many good parts, but the best part had always been Owen. We made up games and shared secret jokes. We told each other stories and collected rocks together. When Owen did something, he'd ask me if I wanted to do it, too. Being four years apart didn't matter.

Until last year.

Owen told Mom and Dad he wanted to see what public school was like. So he went to high school and was gone all day. He made new friends. Then he added *after*-school things like theater and playing right field on the baseball team.

What he subtracted was me. Mom said it sometimes happens as brothers and sisters get older, but I didn't think it'd happen to us.

"Maybe Excited has marbles in her pocket," Owen said. "And she drops them on the track so Scared will slip on them."

I imagined Excited pulling a whole handful of marbles out of her pocket and dropping them one by one.

"Okay. Give me your address," I heard Dad say. "Don't touch him. I'll be right over."

As he put his phone in his pocket, Mom said, "Let me fix you a plate to take with you, Gabe."

"Thanks, but just put it in the fridge," Dad said, pulling on his green warden jacket. "I'll warm it up when I get back. This shouldn't take too long. A woman found a wild rabbit stuck between two wooden pickets in her fence. Guess he tried to jump through and only made it halfway. I hope I don't have to take the fence apart. The lady is already fuming about being late for something."

"Can I come?" I asked.

"But, Emma, I made all your favorite things," Mom said. "And you haven't eaten more than a few bites."

"Thank you, Mom. I love it all, but my stomach's too jumpy to eat." I'd thought about school all summer, but now the big day was *tomorrow*. Little worries were creeping in. What if the other kids knew things that I didn't? What if everyone already had their own friends and didn't want more?

Scared jumped right over those marbles.

"I could pass you tools," I called to Dad. "And the lady will probably be nicer with a kid there."

He paused, his hand on the doorknob, and glanced back at Mom.

She sighed. "All right. We'll save the pie for later. Don't keep her out late, though, Gabe. She has to be up early."

I bolted from my seat so fast that our golden retrievers, Molly and Maggie, started barking like there was an emergency.

"Aren't you coming?" I asked Owen.

He shook his head. "I have to call Jordan. I'm hoping to convince him to try out for soccer with me."

Soccer? When did he decide that?

"You can tell me all about it when you get home," Owen said.

"I hope we can just wiggle the rabbit free," Dad said

as I caught up to him on the front porch. "But let's bring something to put him in, just in case he's injured. I've got a big plastic bin in the barn. That should hold him until we get to the rehab center."

"A bunny in a box!" I said.

Dad smiled. "Rabbit wrangler. That's my job."

Animals are my favorite part of Dad's job. If the rehabilitation center is already closed for the night, Dad might even bring an injured or orphaned animal home with him. Once I came downstairs to breakfast and found a fox kit sleeping in a box by the woodstove. Another morning Mom screamed when she went to put water in the coffeepot and there was a turtle with a cracked shell in a plastic tub in our kitchen sink. A beaver with a bad foot even slept in a cage in our barn one evening. Owen says we run a wildlife bed and breakfast.

Our dogs, Molly and Maggie, are used to it. They just give the newcomer a quick sniff and then accept it as belonging.

Sometimes Dad even lets me come with him to

release an animal back into the wild. As soon as he opens the cage door or the box flaps, a look flashes into that animal's eyes that I can't explain. But it knows it's free. Then there's a rush of wings reaching for the sky or paws racing for the woods and it's gone. The whole thing is over in seconds, but it's the best moment ever.

The worst part of Dad's job is when he catches someone breaking a hunting law. They might have to pay a fine, or even go to jail. Sometimes that conversation happens way out in the woods with no one else around, and the hunter is holding a gun.

Dad would never take me on a call like that, though. Only on quick, simple animal rescues. Like freeing a stuck rabbit from a picket fence and watching him hop away if he's okay or helping him out if he isn't.

I should've known better, though. Rabbits are tricksters. When I was little, I'd always begged my grandfather to tell me stories about Monsieur Lapin, Mr. Rabbit. "It happened once," Pépère would start, and it was like the whole world slowed down to listen. I'd hang on his every word until Monsieur Lapin had cheated and sneaked his way through every near miss and danger.

Little, smart, fast as the wind on a mountaintop, and full of surprises.

Anything is possible with rabbits.

A frightened rabbit can truly be scared to death.

Pépère's stories always began with the words "It happened once." After that, each story took its own twists and turns, like a stream running this way or that way around the rocks, but it always ended with the words "So it was."

When I was little and my grandparents were still alive, Owen and I used to visit Pépère and Mémère every summer at their house, half a day away up north in Quebec, Canada. Dad would drop us off and pick us up a few weeks later.

Even though Owen and I only ever lived with Pépère and Mémère when we visited, Mémère always greeted us with, "You've come home!" And she made it feel like home. I loved belonging there on the farm where Dad grew up.

In the early morning, Pépère would wake Owen and me, and we'd go out in the fields as the sun came up. By midmorning we'd have picked baskets full of vegetables or berries. Then we'd help Mémère bake things to eat and sell.

If I didn't know how to use the sifter or how small to cut the strawberries, Mémère would say, "Watch." She'd move her hands slowly so I could see every movement her fingers made.

At home, that would've felt like work, but it never did at Mémère and Pépère's. As we picked and baked, Pépère would tell us stories. He knew the name of every wild animal in the woods and skies around the farm and spoke to them like friends. He called the animals and birds by their names in French, like Monsieur Castor the beaver, Madame Tortue the turtle, Monsieur Renard the fox, Monsieur Corbeau the crow, Madame Sittelle the nuthatch, and Monsieur Hibou the owl.

My favorite stories were about Monsieur Lapin, a cottontail rabbit who was always getting into trouble. Sometimes he'd trick his way out. Other times he learned a lesson. Those lessons never stuck too well, though. In the next story, he'd be back in trouble. None of the other animals held it against him. It was just who he was.

If a rabbit popped up in the vegetable rows, Pépère would say, "Bonjour, Monsieur Lapin!"

I asked Pépère once why he called *every* rabbit Monsieur Lapin, when really there could only be one. "Every rabbit has some of Monsieur Lapin's magic," he said. "Rabbit magic is a powerful thing."

As Dad drove, I watched out the window and thought how tomorrow would be like the border crossing to Quebec—you drive through the checkpoint and there's a whole different country on the other side. School would change a lot of things. There might be a whole different me on the other side of tomorrow.

I took a deep breath, the way Pépère always did, to pull a story inside me. "It happened once," I said to Dad beside me in the truck. "Monsieur Lapin was running away from that sneaky fox, Monsieur Renard. He jumped through a picket fence and got stuck!"

Dad smiled. He grew up with Pépère's stories, too. "Monsieur Lapin wouldn't need a game warden to free him, would he? He'd trick Monsieur Castor into chewing the fence down with his sharp teeth."

"Or he'd tell Madame Sittelle there were tasty bugs in the wooden pickets," I said. "She and her nuthatch family would come and peck the fence apart, looking for them."

Dad passed a Massachusetts car driving slowly in front of us. Local people call the road we live on "Moose Alley." It's a major road for us, connecting a small town with an even smaller one, right on the edge of the big woods stretching up to Canada.

On the roadside are brushy areas and marshes where moose like to graze. As it gets close to dark or very early in the morning, we get extra cars with out-of-state license plates. That's the time the guidebooks tell you to go looking if you want to see Monsieur Orignal. I've seen moose at all times of day, though. Moose don't read the guidebooks.

Moose Alley doesn't even need a line painted down the middle, because you can drive the whole thirty miles of it, from town to town, and only meet a handful of cars and a few logging trucks. People from away call our part of Maine "the sticks."

Which is true, I guess. We have no shortage of sticks.

Dad turned the truck onto a small dirt road cutting through the woods. It was mostly a camp road. A road you could drive right past and not even see it—but the kind of road where things always seem to happen in Pépère's stories. I breathed in the Christmassy scent of pine and spruce through the open window.

"Okay, Em," Dad said, turning on his headlights to see better. "Help me look for the house now. The lady said it was number sixty-three."

At first, I thought he was kidding. There were hardly any houses, certainly not sixty-three of them, but there were a few numbers nailed to the trees and they seemed to jump ten or more at a time. As we passed each house or camp, I looked for bikes and toys—clues that a kid lived there. There were lots of things I was hoping for tomorrow at school, but making new friends was Number One—maybe I'd even make a best friend. I really wanted to be half of an "and," like you see in books.

Calvin and Hobbes.

Frodo and Sam.

Charlotte and Wilbur.

Maybe we'd solve mysteries together. Or dress up as Thing One and Thing Two for Halloween. Or be copresidents of our own club. And we'd never miss each other, because we'd see each other every day at school.

I'd even made a list.

Emma's Best Friend Checklist
Likes me best.
Likes the things I like.

Shares secret jokes.

Is always on my side.

Lets me be me.

Forgives me when I'm sorry.

I just wrote down everything I missed with Owen. It's not that I didn't have other friends—kids from church and homeschool group—but when you live in a place where the houses are far apart, it takes some planning to see other kids.

Owen had always been there. That's what I missed most, just him being there.

And the worst part was that he *liked* school. Listening to all his stories, I couldn't help wondering if I were missing out on something big.

"This must be it," Dad said.

Up ahead was a clearing with a small gray house and a white picket fence out front. No bikes. No toys. Just an older woman outside holding a broom.

As we got out of the truck, she called to us. "I tried

to poke the rabbit through, but he's wedged in there tight."

Poke him through? I disliked her immediately.

"Don't touch him, ma'am," Dad shouted back pleasantly. He has to be nice to everyone, unless they're breaking the law. I guess there wasn't an actual *law* about poking a rabbit with a broom.

Dad grabbed his toolbox from the back of the truck and gave me the plastic bin and lid.

As I got closer to the fence, I gasped. The rabbit certainly was stuck. His back feet and little puff tail dangled on one side, his head and front feet on the other.

But what shocked me was how small he was. And he wasn't medium brown like a cottontail rabbit or rusty tan like a snowshoe hare in summer. He was a soft honey-gold color with a brown nose and front paws. He seemed to be frozen in fear, except for his little back rising and falling with each breath.

"Well, there's a surprise," Dad said. "Do any of your neighbors have a pet rabbit?"

The woman shook her head. "Not that I know of."

Dad stroked his chin, thinking. "Look, I'm glad to free it, but as a game warden, I only deal with wildlife. You'll need to call your local animal control officer to come get this bunny. They handle pets."

"How long will *that* take?" the woman asked. "I'm supposed to be at a meeting."

"I can give you this bin to keep him in until animal control gets here," Dad said, "but I can't—"

"Let it hop back into the woods," the woman said. "That's where rabbits belong."

"Not *this* rabbit," I said. "He's not wild."

She shot me an angry look. "Well, he's not *my* rabbit!"

I turned to Dad. "You know he doesn't stand a chance in the woods. Not with all those foxes, lynx, and owls."

Dad looked from the lady to the rabbit to me. "Well, there's no need for him to suffer while we figure it out." He leaned down and ran his fingers along the rabbit's sides. "His ribs are too round to go forward, so let's try easing him back the way he came. Em, take the bin and get behind him—but not too close to those hind legs. Even a little bunny's got a kick."

The bin was ridiculously huge for such a tiny rabbit.

"It won't jump up and attack us, will it?" the woman asked.

I saw Dad trying not to smile. "I don't think so, but maybe you'd like to go in your house, ma'am? Just in case. Emma and I are trained rabbit wranglers, but I can't guarantee your safety."

I bit the inside of my lip so I wouldn't giggle. The woman didn't look like she believed Dad, but she took some steps backward anyway.

The rabbit's hind legs were hanging down limp on my side of the fence, but his little tail twitched. My hands were aching to touch him and see if he was as soft as he looked. But I didn't want to scare him even more. "Don't worry," I said, sitting on the ground behind him. "We're here to help you."

Between the pickets, I watched Dad's hands on the rabbit's shoulders. "Come on. Don't fight it," he said, turning the rabbit gently. "You're squeezed in here pretty good. It's gonna take some work to get you out."

The bunny's hind legs started kicking, wiggling him a little more onto my side. "It's helping!" I said. "He's coming!"

"Good! Set the bin on its side so he'll back into it," Dad said. "Then, as soon as he's inside, tip it upright, and throw the lid on."

As I was reaching for the bin, the rabbit gave a mighty kick—and suddenly he was out!

For one second, he looked toward the woods, and I saw it. That same flash of wild in his eyes, seeing freedom. Then he leaped, a funny little jump-spin, landing on my leg. Maybe he was just so happy to be out of the fence that he couldn't help himself.

But it gave me the chance to grab him. "Got him!"

"Great job, Em!" Dad turned to look behind him. "Ma'am, let's call your local—"

But the lady was already in her car.

"Well, what do you expect *me* to do with him?" Dad called.

Her car windows were rolled up, though. She backed out of the driveway and took off down the road.

Dad and I stood there, listening to the sound of her tires crunching the rocks. I held the rabbit against me, his hind legs tucked into the crook of my elbow. He was scared to death, still as stone except for his heart beating wildly under my hand and his whiskers tickling my neck with each panting breath.

"You can't leave him here," I told Dad firmly. "That lady doesn't care what happens to him."

"The nearest animal shelter is in Rangeley, but I'm sure they're closed for the night now." Dad sighed. "I guess we could bring him home and then I could take him to the shelter in the morning."

I tried to act calm, when really, I felt like dancing. I couldn't wait to show Owen! "Can we go *after* school? We rescued him together, and I want to be there."

"I suppose so," Dad said. "But we'd better drive to the store and see if they sell rabbit food."

"And carrots!"

Walking back to the truck, the rabbit hid his face

against my neck, his golden fur surrounded by my red hair. When an animal trusts you, it fills you up with a warm feeling. I rested my cheek against his ears. They were softer than I'd even imagined.

"Are you sure you don't want to put him in the bin?" Dad asked. "He might have ticks or fleas."

"Nope, I'll carry him. And I'll check us both for bugs when we get home."

Dad threw the bin in the back of the truck. "Some days just don't end the way you think they will," he said. "But I guess that's what makes life an adventure."

As we drove back down the road through the woods, the rabbit stared at me. There was a soft look in his eyes. It could've been "thank you" or wonder at the world flying past outside the window.

Finding him felt like a sign—Pépère sending me some rabbit magic to say everything was going to be okay tomorrow.

"Maybe this really *is* Monsieur Lapin," I joked to Dad. "Because he's already tricked *us* into rescuing him and feeding him!"

Dad laughed. "Yes, he has."

As he turned the truck back onto Moose Alley, I pulled in a deep breath. "It happened once. Monsieur Lapin was running away from Monsieur Renard and jumped through a fence and got stuck. So he pretended to be a helpless little pet bunny. He convinced a Maine Game Warden and his daughter to save him, bring him home, and give him a feast of carrots."

Dad nodded. "So it was."

Looking at the rabbit in my arms, my heart hurt, but in a good way. I'd heard of "love at first sight," but I'd always wondered if that was a real thing or just something people said. But that's how it felt—I loved him already.

It's a powerful thing to rescue something.

It changes both of you.

If a rabbit refuses food, it can quickly become an emergency.

At home, Dad set up a cage in the living room. Mom picked some parsley from our garden to add to the carrots, pellets, and Timothy hay that the store clerk had sold us.

I got a plastic bin for the hay and Owen found a water bowl. "Welcome to the Wildlife Bed and Breakfast," he told the bunny.

"This rabbit seems very comfortable with people,"

Mom remarked as she ran her hands over him, looking for injuries.

It was true. The rabbit hadn't squirmed when Dad checked to see if he was a boy or girl (a boy!). Or when I held him and Owen looked through his fur for ticks and fleas. He even stayed calm as Molly and Maggie gave him a quick sniff.

But as soon as I put him in the cage, he crawled on his belly to the corner and then hunched his back, like a furry bowling ball.

I slid a piece of carrot closer.

"Give him some time," Dad said. "He's been through a lot today. He'll probably eat if we leave him alone."

"What if he doesn't?" I asked.

Dad shrugged. "You know how it is with animals, Em. Some things aren't ours to decide. We do our best, but the rest is up to him."

The rabbit stayed hunched in the corner of the cage. Only his little nose moved, opening and closing with each breath.

"Emma and I'll take him to the animal shelter in

Rangeley after school," Dad told Mom. Then he looked at me. "But if he hasn't eaten anything by morning, I want to take him as soon as the shelter opens, okay? Rabbits can go downhill fast if they don't eat."

I nodded. "I bet he'd be happier in my room."

The rabbit's ear closest to me slanted toward the sound of my voice.

"He's fine right where he is," Mom said firmly. "You need a good night's sleep, Emma."

"Yeah," Owen said. "You should get some sleep."

I wrinkled my nose, like he smelled bad. Owen never used to take Mom and Dad's side over mine.

By bedtime, the rabbit still hadn't eaten anything. I pushed the carrot up to his front paws so he didn't even have to stretch to reach it.

He turned his head away.

My heart felt heavy as I went upstairs. The worries about school were boosted up with extra worries about the rabbit. He'd trusted me and now he was alone in a cage.

Scared was pulling ahead of Excited now. In my room,

I emptied my backpack so I could see all my new stuff and give Excited some help. Everything was new: planner, folders, notebooks, water bottle, cute erasers, pencils (colored and regular), pencil sharpener, markers, high-lighters, Post-its (several colors), tissues, lip gloss, pony-tail holder to pull my hair back for gym and recess, and pear-scented hand sanitizer. I had watched online videos of other kids getting ready for school and had bought everything they suggested. I really wished *those* kids were in my class, because they all seemed friendly. None of them lived in Maine, though. So I hoped what they suggested worked here, too.

It had been fun to go back-to-school shopping for the first time. I'd always had some new things to start each year, but I never spent so much time planning what I'd wear. While homeschooling, I'd just see what I felt like wearing that day, but now it seemed important to look interesting but not too different.

For tomorrow, I'd picked out jeans, orange sneakers, and a blue T-shirt with a golden retriever on it. I figured if a kid said something about my shirt, I could start a conversation about Molly and Maggie instead of just saying "Thanks."

I wished I could wear the leather boots I had bought, but though mornings were almost cold enough for frost, afternoons were still hot. In homeschool, I could've just changed with the weather, but now I had to pick something to last the whole day.

It was exciting to have so many new things, but when I changed into my pajamas and shut off the light, Scared was waiting for me. What if I didn't know something important? Or I did something embarrassing like forget to zip my backpack and everything spilled out on the bus? Or I accidentally squirted my new hand sanitizer all over my new jeans and reeked of pears for the rest of the day?

Pretty soon, I was worrying about *everything*.

Outside, a fox barked in the woods. It always sounds like an angry scream. Maybe Monsieur Renard had discovered that Monsieur Lapin had escaped him yet again.

I wished I knew if the rabbit had eaten. What if he was scared listening to the fox bark, and thinking I'd abandoned him? That he'd just traded one way of being stuck for another?

I couldn't bear the idea that I'd rescued him, only to have him die alone and afraid in our living room. I grabbed my flashlight and tiptoed down the dark stairs so I wouldn't wake Mom and Dad. The rabbit looked wary as my flashlight beam touched him in the corner of the cage. The carrot was right where I'd left it at his feet.

The rabbit kicked a little as I slid my hand under him and pulled him out of the cage, but he calmed down as I held him against my chest. He was small enough to hold with one arm, so I dropped the carrot, the parsley— droopy now—and my flashlight into my bathrobe pocket. I set the water bowl into his hay bin and carried every- thing upstairs.

Maybe Dad was right that some things aren't ours to decide, but other things *are.*

After I closed my bedroom door behind me, I set the rabbit on the braided rug in front of my dresser. I wished I could just let him hop around my room all night, but rabbits are chewers. So I dumped the clothes out of my pink plastic laundry basket and lined the bottom with a towel to make it comfy. Then I put the water bowl, food, and hay bin in the corners of the basket and pushed it up beside my bed. We'd done that when Molly and Maggie were tiny puppies so we could reach down and pat them if they whimpered in the night.

It seemed like a perfect plan, but when I turned around, the rug was empty. Two back feet and a puff tail were disappearing under my dresser.

Uh-oh. I dropped to my knees. The rabbit was way underneath. He gave a tiny sneeze. "Sorry," I said. "Did you find some dust bunnies to play with?"

He wiggled out, and I tried to catch him. *Rabbit Wrangler to the rescue!* He was as fast as a cartoon character, though. He'd hop in one direction and, just as I reached for him, suddenly he'd twist his body almost in half and race the other way. It took three tries and few scratches before I got my palm on his back. He flattened himself on the floor, and I wrapped my hands around his middle.

Carrying him to the laundry basket, I kissed the top of his head. His ears were so warm. I wanted to cuddle him, but it was almost midnight now, and my alarm was set for six. "Time for bed."

In the laundry basket, he sniffed the plastic sides and pushed his nose into the vents. He dug into a corner and bunched up the towel. Then he rose on his hind legs and put his front paws on the top edge of the basket. He wasn't heavy enough to tip it over, but one back foot went into his water dish. I couldn't help giggling.

Then he gave a big hop—right out of the basket.

Oh no!

Two long hops and he was under my nightstand. He started to chew the cord to my lamp.

"No!" As I reached for him, he went under my bed.

Then I had an idea. I took everything out of the laundry basket and sat on the edge of my bed, holding the basket upside down on my knees. I waited until the rabbit came out from under the bed. I pretended I wasn't paying attention to him, but the next time he hopped past, I dropped the laundry basket over him, like a big pink plastic tent. He had plenty of air with all the vents, and he couldn't hop out.

Lifting one edge of the basket, I slid the hay bin and water bowl underneath. I pushed the carrot and the droopy parsley through a vent.

But as I climbed into bed, the laundry basket started moving across the floor. The rabbit was pushing it with his nose! His water would probably get spilled, but I smiled anyway as I turned off the light.

I listened to the soft scrape of the laundry basket on the floor. Tomorrow everything would change. A yellow bus would stop at the end of our driveway for me, and Dad and I'd take the rabbit to the shelter after school. But for this warm, dark moment, none of that had happened yet.

I heard a clomping sound, like two wood blocks softly hitting each other. I clicked on my flashlight and saw some of the parsley wiggling from the rabbit's mouth. He was eating! I was so relieved that I laughed.

I wondered if he'd still be under the laundry basket when I woke up. Maybe he'd figure a way out and I'd find him in my closet or under my bed. Or beneath my dresser playing with the dust bunnies.

Or if he really *were* Monsieur Lapin, he'd trick us all. He'd squeeze out from under the laundry basket and spring up and away through an open window with quite a story to tell the other animals.

"Silly Monsieur Lapin," they'd say. "Why are you always in trouble?"

But he'd grin, knowing *he* was the one with a full belly of parsley and carrots.

"Good night, Monsieur Lapin," I whispered, turning off my flashlight.

Most rabbits are happiest in bonded pairs or groups.

The next morning, I couldn't remember why my alarm was going off. Then it hit me. It was the first day of school!

All the thinking and planning was over. The day was finally here. As I leaped out of bed, I noticed the upside-down laundry basket, wedged between my dresser and nightstand. Through the vents, I could see the outline of bunny ears.

There were lots of little rabbit poops to clean up, but I didn't care. His food was gone, and the water bowl was empty! I lifted the laundry basket so he could run around my room while I cleaned up and got dressed.

As I brushed my hair, I practiced smiling. It's hard to get just the right amount of smile—not too crazy-big and desperate, but enough to show I'm friendly. "Hi, I'm Emma," I said softly to myself in the mirror. "I'm new here."

May as well just admit it. Most of these kids had probably known each other since kindergarten. And my red hair stands out right away. There's no melting into any crowd. In fact, it's always easy to find me in a group photo—just look for my hair.

It was thrilling to be like all those other kids heading off to school today, even if I was faking it a bit. Of course, I'd miss the freedom. With homeschooling, if I got right to work first thing in the morning and stuck to it without many breaks, I could be all done with my lessons by lunchtime and have the whole afternoon to myself to go kayaking or hiking or read.

Freedom can be lonely, though. It would be great to have a built-in group of kids to belong to. Maybe Owen would even feel lonesome without *me* for a change! It'd be nice not to explain, too. When people asked me, "Where do you go to school?" the answer would just be a name, not a whole conversation.

Behind me in the mirror, I saw the rabbit jump into my trash can. He looked so funny with just his ears showing.

"Emma!" I heard Mom yell up the stairs. "Breakfast!"

"Coming!" I grabbed my backpack and a rock from my collection on the windowsill. A long time ago, Mom took Owen and me on a homeschool field trip to the Audubon Society. The gift shop had pretty "Inspiration Stones" for sale, each one with a word engraved on it, like *Trust*, *Create*, and *Love*. I wanted to buy one, but Owen said we could easily make our own. So every time I went somewhere special, I brought a rock home and wrote a word or phrase on it with a permanent marker.

Discover.

Imagine.

Courage.

Kindness.

Good Luck.

Keep Going.

Wish.

You Got This!

"You got this!" I said out loud, putting the rock in my pocket. Then I scooped the rabbit out of the trash can. In my arms, he tucked his head under my chin and a feeling hit me like a blast of fire. I'd do anything to protect him.

"I wish you could come to school with me today," I whispered into his fur.

In the kitchen, Dad and Owen looked up from their plates of scrambled eggs and toast. Usually, Owen would be gone before me, but high school didn't start until tomorrow.

"I knew you'd have him!" Owen said. "Mom was about to tear the living room apart looking for that rabbit."

Mom glanced at me from the corner of her eye. "Emma, didn't I tell you to leave him in the cage?"

"I was so worried about him that I couldn't sleep," I said. "I've named him Monsieur Lapin. Lapi for short."

"Please don't get attached to him, honey," Mom said. "He must be someone's pet."

She was probably right. And if Maggie and Molly had gotten lost and someone found them, I'd want them back.

It was too late to tell me not to get attached, though.

"He ate all his food." As I opened the refrigerator, Lapi startled at the cold air. I touched a carrot green to his nose and he took a nibble. "See, Dad? He's eating!"

"Okay," Dad said. "I'll wait for you to get home from school before we take him to the shelter."

"He doesn't like the cage, though," I said.

"We still have the exercise pen from when Maggie

and Molly were puppies," Dad said. "Maybe he'd like that better. It's bigger and not so closed in. It's out in the barn. I'll bring it in and set it up for him before I go to work."

"Until then, he needs to go in the cage so you can eat breakfast, Emma," Mom said. "And wash your hands."

I felt bad putting Lapi in the cage, but he didn't seem to mind it as much as he had last night.

"So who's ahead?" Owen asked as I sat down beside him at the table. "Scared or Excited?"

"Excited has been training all summer for this day," I said. "Scared forgot to eat breakfast."

He smiled. "Well, if Scared starts catching up, just remember that the beginning is the hardest."

The beginning is the hardest, I repeated in my head as I ate.

"Don't forget to put your name on all your work. You'll lose points if you do," Owen said. "And when your teacher tells you an assignment, be sure to write it down. At home, you could just ask Mom if you forgot something. But at school, you're expected to hear it once and remember it."

Write everything down. It was new to be so responsible for myself, but I loved my assignment notebook—all those blank pages ready to be filled up with important things.

"And don't feel bad if you don't understand something," Owen continued. "Just ask. Most kids are nice and will help you if you need it. Pick your first friends carefully, though. Sometimes that's who you end up with for good. And other kids don't give you too many chances before they write you off as strange."

Now at the last minute he was full of advice about school? I knew Owen was trying to help, but he was telling me things that I hadn't even known to worry about!

As I came over to say good-bye, Lapi pushed his nose between the bars of the cage. "I'll see you this afternoon," I promised, giving his fur a little rub.

Outside on the front porch, Mom took my photo. I grinned and struck a pose with my brand-new backpack at my feet and my arms up in the air in a big V.

"Have a great day!" Mom said, giving me a hug.

I hoisted my backpack onto my shoulder. It felt light, though when I came home, it would probably be full of books, like Owen's last year.

I knew I'd get tired of having homework, but for today, it felt grown-up, too.

"Hold out your hand." Owen reached into his pocket. "I have something for you, but don't look at it now, okay? Read it when you need it."

I curled my fingers around the little rock he placed on my palm. I slid it into my jeans pocket with You Got This!

"Thanks!" I said. "See you this afternoon!"

Walking down the driveway, my toes were getting cold and I could smell a hint of woodsmoke on the breeze. I huffed hard to see my breath.

In our yard, our apple tree was loaded with apples. Some had already dropped in a pile around the trunk. A few sunflowers were still peeking above the deer fence in the garden. And across Moose Alley, the trees were turning. Some trees turn all at once, from bright green to hazy yellow-green, then bright yellow. Others turn in patches, one flashy red or orange branch at a time. The pines and spruces couldn't care less. They stay green all year round. Today the skinny spruce trees with their pointy tops reminded me of sharpened pencils, like the brand-new ones in my backpack.

I heard the bus coming before I saw it. Excited tossed a banana peel onto the road and Scared went down hard.

As the bus stopped in front of me, I felt my muscles tense, bracing myself, like I did before diving into the lake for the first time and hitting cold water. I waved to my family once more before climbing the steps.

"Hi, I'm Emma." I smiled at the driver. "I'm new here."

He nodded and smiled back. "Good morning, Emma."

I also smiled at the kids in the front seats, but they were little and talking to each other. Too young to be best friend material.

I chose an empty seat in the middle and touched the lumps of my pocket. You Got This! And—?

I wanted to look, but I didn't want to use up the surprise.

The bus was noisy and bumpy. Riding down familiar old Moose Alley didn't feel familiar, even though it was all the same hills and dips, twists and turns.

The grass on the roadside looked tired, long and wheat-colored, spotted with blue coneflowers, orange Indian paintbrushes, and white Queen Anne's lace. Power line wires sagged between the poles, and above the tree-tops, the mountains peeked around each other, all points and folds, like a huge origami crown, made by someone who didn't really know how.

We crossed the little bridge over the river. Same bridge, same river full of rocks, but today it felt like passing through that Canada checkpoint, an ending and a beginning at the same time.

"Is that your real hair?" a small voice asked.

I turned to see two little girls in the seat behind me, probably first graders. They were sitting so close together that they had to be best friends. They even had the same coat, one in pink, one in purple.

"Yes, it's my real hair." I smiled, even though I get tired of complete strangers talking about my hair. But these girls looked cute together, and they gave me hope that maybe there was a best friend waiting for me, too.

"I like it," the girl in pink replied. "It looks like oranges."

"Uh, thanks." She meant it as a good thing, but who wants to look like fruit?

"You could be a carton of orange juice for Halloween!" the one in purple said.

The girl in pink nodded. "Yeah! You could put a straw in your hair."

They weren't trying to make me feel bad but some conversations are actually worse than being quiet. "Hmm. I'll think about that," I said and turned back around.

One day this will be easy, I promised myself. *I'll get on the bus and won't feel like a new kid. And I'll have a best friend, too.*

The girls were still talking about Halloween as the bus went through downtown. Out front of the hiking store stood two scruffy-looking men wearing shorts and boots, weighted down with enormous backpacks— probably Appalachian Trail thru-hikers come into town for supplies. In the market, you can smell those hikers a couple aisles away. Dad sometimes picks them up when they're hitchhiking to and from the trail. Even if they're smelly, I love to hear their stories. One man from Tennessee played songs for me on his ukulele while we drove him back to the trail.

Dad doesn't mind the AT hikers so much, because they're usually well prepared. It's the day hikers who start off at three o'clock in the afternoon in flip-flops who frustrate him. Sometimes he has to go get them when it gets dark and their family gets worried or they call for help. I'm sure he gives them a stern talking-to about hiking boots and flashlights on the way down the mountain.

The bus passed the marina, the post office, the real estate office with its side-by-side American and Canadian flags, the bank, the coffee shop with cars and ATVs parked out front for breakfast, the library, and the ice cream shop (with a sign in the window, "Closing on Columbus Day"). As the bus turned off Main Street, I felt my heart going into hyper-speed. I couldn't tell if it was Excited or Scared speeding it up, though.

The bus pulled into the long half-circle driveway in front of the school. The building itself looked like a huge brick box with a flat roof and small rectangular windows. A banner hung above the doorway that said, "Welcome to Lakeview Elementary School, Home of the Lakers!" Lakers was a funny name, not fierce like most school mascots: Bobcats or Bears or Tigers.

Watch out! We're the mighty, mighty—Lake.

I was glad, though. A lake felt familiar, calming, and gentle.

A few buses were lined up in front of the school. Out back were ball fields, and on the side were some gardens in raised beds with a little homemade greenhouse. A deer fence surrounded the garden area, but I could see a hole under the fence where some animal had dug under. I smiled, imagining the story Pépère might tell.

It happened once that Monsieur Lapin saw a school at the edge of the woods. Then he noticed something green growing in the garden. "I'll go have myself a look," he thought, twitching his nose. "And a taste!"

He'd trick some other animal into doing the work, though. Maybe he'd come upon stinky black-and-white Madame Moufette. *"I hear there are tasty grubs under that fence,"* Monsieur Lapin would say. *"I'll come back later and eat them."*

"You go on," Madame Moufette would say, waiting for him to leave. Then she'd dig and dig until she'd made a big hole and not find a single grub. *"When I see Monsieur Lapin, I'll give him a big spray with my tail!"* she'd grumble, waddling away to the woods.

Monsieur Lapin would come back later and have a good big hole already made for him, right into that delicious garden.

The bus stopped with a screech of brakes. "Everyone out!" the driver said. "Have a great first day!"

So it was. Just thinking about Pépère and his stories made me feel braver. I picked up my backpack and followed the other students up the bus aisle and down the walkway. There were kids everywhere—kindergartners to fifth graders, rushing and laughing and talking really loudly to each other.

Before I stepped inside the school, I decided I had earned a peek at Owen's rock. I stepped off to the side of the walkway to let the other kids pass by.

He'd written "Be" on one side. I imagined what could be on the other side.

Be Brave?

Be Happy?

Be Strong?

Be—I squeezed the rock tightly in my hand before turning it over.

Yourself.

> **Rabbits are naturally curious. Once comfortable with their nearby environment, they'll want to explore beyond it.**

My heart bounced inside me as I was carried along in the river of kids going down the hallway. Lakeview Elementary School looked different than it did when Mom and I visited last summer. The halls had been empty then with only a few things on the walls. Now there were bright colors everywhere, and kids seemed to fill every available space, all talking at once.

Don't trip or you'll be a goner! I thought as I made my way past each decorated classroom door.

"Our New Pack!" said one door, with kids' names written on construction paper crayons.

"Second Grade Is Sweet!" said another, with names on cupcake shapes.

"Emma!" a voice said. "Is that you?"

I turned and smiled. Even though she was younger than me, Shonna and I had been in homeschool group together two years ago. It was so nice to see someone I knew that I wanted to hug Shonna, except there were too many kids in the way. "Hi! I'm going to public school this year," I said.

"I can't believe you're here!" Shonna said. "Who's your teacher?"

"Ms. Hutton."

"Come on. I'll take you there." Shonna hoisted her yellow backpack onto her shoulder and walked confidently around kids down the hallway. It felt weird to follow someone younger than me—especially since the little kids had followed *me* in homeschool group—but it was a relief not to do this alone.

Shonna paused at a door near the end of the hallway. "This is it!" The door was decorated like a tree with construction paper owls and the words "Look Whooo's in Fifth Grade!"

"Emma" was on a cute blue owl with big eyes outlined in green.

Yes, this was really happening.

"Thanks, Shonna!" I said, but she was already being swallowed up by the crowd of kids in the hall.

Stepping inside the room felt like coming downstairs on Christmas morning. The big whiteboard was outlined in stars and someone had written on it, "Welcome, Fifth Graders!"

It seemed like everywhere I turned there were so many exciting things. Colorful paper lanterns hung from the ceiling, and there were leafy plants on the windowsill. Between the big windows were bookcases full of books.

I recognized some of my favorites displayed on top: *Diary of a Wimpy Kid*, *Smile*, *The One and Only Ivan*, and *Because of Winn-Dixie*. It was comforting to see them, like I already had a few friends in the room.

Over in the corner, a plastic toy chest held a jumble of playground equipment. One ball had the words "Hutton Kickball" on it. I'd heard of kickball, but I'd never played it before. Maybe I could look up the rules online when I got home.

The desks were pushed together into groups of four. Every desk had a new pencil and a nametag on it. I found "Emma" right away and put my backpack on the chair.

My own desk! I'd be sitting next to "Jack," and across from "Leah" and "Iris." I practiced their names in my head *Jack, Leah, Iris. Jack, Leah, Iris.*

We all had four-letter names! That seemed like a good sign. I opened my backpack and pretended to be busy while the other kids were milling around.

"Everyone, please put on your nametag and gather on the rug," said Ms. Hutton. She had chin-length blonde hair and wore a pretty gray skirt with a white sweater and a chunky orange necklace.

I took off my jacket and stuck "Emma" on my shirt, careful not to cover up the golden retriever.

Sitting on the rug with the other kids, I wiggled my toes inside my sneakers to keep the rest of me still. I couldn't believe I was really here. Excited had turned on a burst of speed, leaving Scared coughing in the dust.

Maybe one of these kids was my future best friend? I smiled so I'd look friendly in case anyone looked at me. A few girls wore dresses and skirts, but others were in jeans like me. A girl with long brown hair in a ponytail was twirling her necklace around her finger. A blonde girl with glasses had her pen with her. I hoped I hadn't made a mistake by leaving mine in my backpack.

Fifth graders came in more sizes than I expected. I was relieved to see I was in the middle, not the biggest or tallest or shortest, either. No other girls had red hair, but one boy did. His hair was blonder than mine, but still, it was nice not to be the only one.

"Welcome to your last year of elementary school!" Ms. Hutton said.

The kids cheered, so I did, too.

"Let me start by telling you a little about myself." Ms. Hutton smiled. "But I'll do it in a fun way. It's a game called Two Truths and a Lie, where I'll tell you three things, but only two of them are true. When I'm done, you'll guess which one's the lie."

My teacher was going to lie? I looked around to see if anyone else thought that was shocking. The other kids were smiling.

"My family likes to hike in the White Mountains," Ms. Hutton said. "I have a pet cat named Sirius Black from my son's favorite book series. And I've never been downhill skiing."

Never been skiing? That had to be the lie. We were surrounded by mountains and ski areas.

"As I repeat them, raise your hand for the one you think is the lie," Ms. Hutton said.

I raised my hand for the skiing statement, along with almost everyone else.

"Now I'll reveal the answers!" Ms. Hutton held up a big framed photo of her with her husband and two teen-aged kids on a mountaintop with layers of blue and purple mountains in the background. "My family loves to hike. So that statement is true," she said. "Here we are at the top of Mount Washington in July."

Dad would approve of their hiking boots and poles. I couldn't wait to tell her that I like to hike, too!

She picked up another photo and turned it around to show us a little dog. "This is our dog, Baxter."

Wait. What? Baxter wasn't the name, and she'd said she had a cat! "You've never been skiing?" I asked loudly.

The whole class looked at me.

"That's right, Emma!" Ms. Hutton said. "But let's remember to raise your hand when you want to say something, okay?"

I felt my face burning red. I had certainly seen school kids on TV raise their hands, but I'd never had to do that myself. And I didn't like being in trouble.

"I've never been downhill skiing, because I lived in Georgia for most of my life," Ms. Hutton explained.

"In fact, before we moved here five years ago, I'd only ever seen snow a few times!" Ms. Hutton smiled. "Another true thing about me is that I've been a teacher for twelve years. And I have to admit that fifth grade is my favorite grade to teach. Fifth graders are independent, have a great sense of humor, and are wonderful problem solvers. They are compassionate and care deeply about things."

I lifted my head higher with each nice thing Ms. Hutton said.

"And this is Ms. Martel. She'll be helping out at some times during the day."

I looked behind me to another woman. She was younger than Ms. Hutton, with brown hair and lots of freckles. She waved to us.

I waved back. No one else did, so I put my hand down fast.

"I know we'll have a great year together," Ms. Hutton continued. "Now I want you to get to know each other. So find your seats and I'll tell you what we're going to do next."

At our group of desks, the other three kids immediately started unpacking their backpacks. So I opened mine and took out my assignment notebook and a cute panda eraser. I wanted to be ready as soon as Ms. Hutton started telling us what we needed to do.

Suddenly, it felt weird that this was real. I'd been imagining and thinking about today for so long that the waiting part seemed to go on forever and the real part was coming too fast. I touched my pocket to feel the bump of the two rocks.

You Got This!
Be Yourself.

"Hi, I'm Emma," I said to the kids around me, giving my friendliest, but not crazy-big, smile. "I'm new here."

Leah and Iris said hi back. They both looked nice. Leah had short blonde hair and wore bright blue glasses. Iris's brown hair was held back with a green headband.

"Where did you come from?" Iris asked.

"I'm new to this *school*," I said. "But I've lived on Moose Alley my whole life."

"Oh," Leah said. "How do you like it here compared to your old school?"

I didn't want to tell them I'd been homeschooled just yet. In books and movies, homeschool kids are usually super quirky. I didn't want them to expect me to be like that. Owen had said other kids don't give you too many chances. "I like it so far," I said instead.

"It's a golden retriever," Jack said, looking at my shirt. His hands were on his thighs, but his fingers were twitching, like a secret wave.

"I have two goldens at home," I said, glad to change the subject. "Do you have any—?"

But Ms. Hutton clapped her hands to get our attention. "Okay, now that you've had a minute to get settled, *you* are going to play Two Truths and a Lie with your seatmates. Remember to come up with two true things that the other kids in your group won't already know about you and one lie. I'll give you some time to think and then we'll play the game."

Leah, Iris, and Jack barely knew *anything* about me, so that part would be easy. I opened my new notebook to write down my statements. The truths seemed easier. I'd already mentioned my dogs. I could tell about Lapi, but he wasn't mine to keep and I didn't want to explain that.

So I wrote: *We once had a beaver in our barn.*

That was true and seemed different enough that the other kids might not believe it.

I've hatched frogs in our bathroom at home. It was a home-school science project, but I didn't have to tell that part. Most kids like animals, so they might find that interesting.

And now a lie. *I love dill pickles.* When my family eats out at a restaurant and they put a pickle on my plate, I always give it to Mom.

Iris went first. "I'm afraid of elevators. When I was six, I broke my wrist falling out of a tree. I'm allergic to tomatoes."

Leah rolled her eyes. "That's too easy for me. Emma and Jack can guess."

"Tomatoes give you hives," Jack said. "Last year, you had to go to the emergency room during lunch."

As the new kid, I could see I was at a big disadvantage in this game.

Iris huffed. "You're supposed to guess the *lie*, Jack."

"I think the lie is elevators," I said.

"Emma's right," Iris said. "I actually love elevators. Especially the ones that have a glass side so you can see out as you're going up. Climbing stairs is so boring. And I did really break my wrist when I was six. In fact, I still have my cast! Your turn, Leah."

"I had a hard time thinking of things you wouldn't know," she said to Iris. Then she smiled at me. "Iris and I have known each other since we were babies."

Leah and Iris acted like a team already. That was exactly what I missed with Owen. And what I wanted again.

Leah cleared her throat. "I stepped on a bee this summer. I'm a vegetarian. My toenails have green polish on them." She smiled. "And don't bother looking, because I'm wearing sneakers!"

"Was it a wasp?" Jack asked.

"I don't know. But if that's your guess, you're wrong," Leah said. "I did step on a bee. And it hurt so much that I didn't look to see what kind it was."

"Wasps can sting more than once," Jack said. "Social wasps give off a chemical when threatened that tells the rest of the colony to attack. If—"

"Jack, remember to stay on topic," a voice said.

I turned to see Ms. Martel making a spinning motion with her finger. "Move on," she said quietly to Jack.

Jack closed his mouth.

"Remember you can write yourself some cue cards if you need help staying focused," Ms. Martel said and walked over to the next set of desks.

I was pretty sure Jack had some special needs. I had met kids with special needs before because that's one reason kids sometimes get homeschooled. I was wondering what else Jack was going to say about wasps, though. We get them around our apple trees a lot, and as Dad says, the better you understand an animal, the easier it is to keep you both safe.

"Um, is the lie about nail polish?" I asked.

"Yes!" Leah said. "I'm wearing hot pink!"

"You're a vegetarian?" Iris asked. "Since when?"

"Since about a month ago," Leah said. "But I've wanted to for a long time."

Iris looked shocked. Maybe they weren't as close as I had thought? Best friends would probably know you'd changed to be vegetarian.

Or maybe they had been best friends when they were little, but were just regular friends now? And each open to a *new* best friend?

"Your turn, Emma," Leah said.

I didn't want to read my statements in order, so I started with the lie. "I love pickles. I've hatched frogs in our bathroom at home. We once had a beaver in our barn."

"The beaver, definitely!" Iris said. "That's just weird."

"It's weird enough to be *true*," Leah said. "I'm guessing frogs."

"Frogs in the bathroom is disgusting," Iris said. "Ugh. Can you imagine slimy frog eggs right next to where you brush your teeth!"

Leah shivered, and I felt the smile slipping off my face. I hadn't kept the frog eggs in the *sink*. They were in a glass bowl on the shelf. Mom wanted them in a place where I could wash my hands easily after changing their water.

"Pickles," Jack said.

I opened my mouth to say yes, but the word got stuck in my throat. "The beaver is true," I said, giving myself a moment to think. "My dad's a game warden, and the beaver was one that he rescued. It was in a cage in our barn overnight because the rehab center wasn't open yet."

"Okay, that's not weird. It's great," Leah said. "What's the lie?"

I hesitated. It was just a game, a small thing, and really, what would it matter? I'd be with these kids every day for a whole school year. I needed to get off to a good start. I didn't want them to think I was weird or, worse, disgusting.

"The frogs," I said.

"I knew it!" Iris said. "No one would keep slimy frog eggs in their bathroom."

"I would," Jack said.

I forced a smile. At least someone was on my side.

"I don't like pickles," Leah said. "So if I get one, you can have it, Emma. Okay, Jack. Your turn."

"I learned to read when I was three years old. I like Legos. I don't like animals."

"That's too easy," Iris said. "You always talk about animals. So the lie is that you don't like them."

"You win!" Jack said.

"You learned to read when you were three?" I asked. "That's amazing!"

"*Dr. Seuss's ABC* was my first book!" Jack said. "'BIG A, little a—'"

Ms. Hutton clapped her hands. "Did you find out some fun things about each other? Now we're going to take that activity and make it bigger. It will be your first fifth grade assignment!"

I opened my assignment notebook to today's date, which I had outlined in purple hearts.

"You'll work in your groups of four. Each group will prepare a short presentation introducing us to everyone in your group using Two Truths and a Lie. On presentation day, you will introduce us to your seatmates by telling us three things about them, but only two will be true. The class will guess the lie."

"Is there a prize if we guess right?" a boy asked.

Ms. Hutton smiled. "The prize will be getting to know your classmates."

"Aww," the boy said. "I was hoping for chocolate."

"Finally you'll reveal the answers," Ms. Hutton said. "Please bring some props or pictures with you, just like I did with my photo of my family hiking. I've saved one bulletin board and a big table that we can use to display things."

I looked where she pointed. The bulletin board said, "Ms. Hutton's Fabulous Fifth Graders!" surrounded with owls with our names on them, just like on the classroom door.

"Your groups will present to the class on Friday," Ms. Hutton said. "It'll be a fun way for us to wrap up our first week together. Any questions?"

Iris raised her hand. "Can we make a video for our presentation? Some of the things I want to show are too big to bring into school."

Ms. Hutton hesitated, but then she said, "Sure! Be creative, as long as it follows the format of Two Truths and a Lie."

Iris leaned across her desk to whisper to Leah, Jack, and me, "Video is easier than doing it in person. Leah, you and I can say the statements about each other. Jack and Emma can work together, too. Then we'll just put it all together at the end. It'll save us time."

"Sounds good," Leah said.

Wait. What? It was decided? We were supposed to work together, and I hadn't even said anything yet! I tried not to let the disappointment show on my face.

I had a feeling it'd be harder to work with Jack. But I couldn't say that. I didn't want to hurt his feelings or make Iris and Leah mad.

So I nodded. "Sounds good," I lied.

A pet rabbit's diet should consist mostly of grass hay.

School definitely had some fun parts, but it was exhausting. In homeschool, Mom had always given me a list of things to do every day, and I had to finish each one—no matter how long or short it took. But here, school was by the clock.

Just when I was getting into science, it was time to switch to math. It seemed like I was always putting books away in my desk and taking others out. And yet, even with all that switching, whenever I looked at the clock, I couldn't believe more time hadn't passed. And it was hard to pay attention after a while. I'd wondered and planned so much for my first day and now I didn't know if I'd last through it.

It was a relief when it was finally lunchtime. Now I could work on making a friend!

As we lined up to go to lunch, Ms. Hutton said, "Remember that as fifth graders, you no longer have assigned seats in the cafeteria. The back tables are all yours and you can choose whatever seat you want."

Everyone cheered, so I did, too.

Stepping into the cafeteria, I was nearly knocked over by how loud it was. Kids were talking and laughing and banging trays down at their seats. It was like they had been saving up the noise all morning.

And it smelled like lots of foods mixed up together, like French fries and pizza, with a dash of tuna.

There were lots of rules—where to pick up your silverware, how to order, which line to get in for different things. I could barely tell where each line ended, and

I accidentally got into the drinks line twice! Even so, I forgot to get a straw. The Lakeview Elementary School cafeteria seemed like a huge kid traffic jam.

When I finally got up to the lunch counter to choose what to eat, I didn't even know what some of the foods were. So I picked a square of pizza, carrot sticks, an apple, and a plop of what I hoped was chocolate pudding.

I shouldn't have picked the apple, though. It wobbled on my tray every time I moved, making it hard to walk very fast.

Being able to sit anywhere might have seemed special to the other fifth graders, but whoever made that rule wasn't thinking about new kids. Standing in the middle of the cafeteria holding my blue plastic tray, I didn't know where to go. Leah and Iris were the only girls I'd really met so far and they were already sitting at a full table of girls with no room for me.

Just sit down. Maybe you'll make a friend. I took a deep breath and froze a smile on my face, walking through the maze of tables to the first empty seat.

When I got there, I saw a notebook on the chair. "Sorry," a girl said. "That seat's saved."

The next empty seat had a baseball cap on it.

The longer I walked around, the more seats were filling up. I wanted to hide my tray somewhere and sneak back to the classroom, where I had my own desk. But I didn't think we were allowed to do that.

Finally I picked one of the empty tables in the far back of the cafeteria with no one else.

The first day is the hardest. I'll bring my own lunch tomorrow. Then I can sit with someone faster.

But as I was sitting down, my foot hit the table leg and my apple wobbled right over the lip of my tray! It bounced once on the table, dropped to the floor, and rolled under the table next to me.

I knew I should find it and throw it away. But climbing under tables wouldn't be a good first impression. Owen had said other kids didn't give you too many chances before they wrote you off as weird.

I took a bite of my pizza, hoping no one had noticed the apple. Maybe I could find it after lunch was over.

At least I had something to do now—eat. But even that's hard when you feel bad. The pizza crust was really chewy and the milk didn't help wash it down.

Jack set his tray at the seat beside me. "School ends at two-forty."

"Hi, Jack." I glanced at the clock above the serving window. How could there still be so much time left? I imagined Mom at home. She often did her own work as a freelance designer in the morning between our lessons, but now was when Mom usually made herself a cup of tea and we read together. I wondered what she'd do today.

And what was Lapi doing? I couldn't help feeling jealous that Mom and Lapi got to spend the day together.

I looked down at my tray. I was glad to have Jack beside me but also concerned. Owen had said to pick your first friends carefully, and Jack didn't seem to have many friends, either. I didn't necessarily want to be super popular, but I wanted the other kids to get to know me before they decided.

None of those other kids had saved me a seat, though.

Another boy came over to our table. He was wearing a camo T-shirt and looked like he couldn't wait for lunch to be over, either. "Hey, Jack," he said.

I smiled at him. "Hi. I'm Emma."

He nodded. "I'm Dustin."

"Nice shirt." I couldn't think of one other thing to say, but maybe he'd say, "You, too."

"Thanks," Dustin said and started eating.

Glancing around at the other kids in the cafeteria, I felt like our table was the Leftovers Table. Leah and Iris were laughing with four other girls. Watching them, I couldn't help wishing I was over there.

From the corner of my eye, I saw an apple shoot past my foot. It rolled across the floor.

Uh-oh. Was that mine?

Dustin kicked it. The apple went skittering past me, like a little red soccer ball, and under another table. That table started laughing. A girl at that table kicked it, and the apple rolled off toward another table.

I looked at the teachers patrolling the room. They

were all busy talking to each other or helping the littlest kids tie shoes or open milk cartons.

I could feel my face getting hot. Even though I hadn't done anything wrong on purpose, I'd started it.

I picked up a carrot stick from my tray. "My rabbit likes carrots," I said, pretending we were just having a regular conversation and I hadn't seen the apple.

"Carrots are high in sugar and should only be fed to rabbits as an occasional treat," Jack replied.

"Really?" I felt awful that I'd given them to Lapi. But *occasional* doesn't mean *never*.

"Grass hay is their main food. It helps wear their teeth down," Jack continued. "If rabbits don't wear their teeth down, they just grow and grow."

I opened my mouth to say that we had given Lapi hay, but a woman's voice said, "How's your first day been, Jack?"

I turned to see Ms. Martel behind me.

"Emma has a rabbit," Jack replied.

"I asked how your first day has been, Jack," she said. "What do you say when—?"

He sighed. "My first day has been good. Emma has a rabbit."

"That's great!" Ms. Martel smiled. "I'm glad you're having a good first day. And how fun that Emma has a pet rabbit. I'm sure that gives you a lot to talk about. What is the rabbit's name?"

"Monsieur Lapin," I said. "It comes from stories my pépère used to tell me about a trickster rabbit."

"Silly rabbit," Jack said. "Trix are for kids!"

I giggled. I didn't know if he'd meant to tell a joke, but it was *funny*.

"Whose apple is this?" a loud voice asked.

One of the teachers was holding my apple by the tiny stem. It wasn't round anymore. It had chunks missing from being kicked around the room.

There was a lot of snickering. I opened my mouth to say it had been an accident. But no words would come out. My heart tightened, waiting for some kid to point at me.

But no one did.

"Don't leave a mess for someone else to clean up," the

teacher snapped, throwing what was left of my apple in a trash can. "You can get ready for recess now—just be sure all your trash gets in the can."

I was so grateful lunch was over that I was one of the first kids to take their tray to the trash cans. There were several different-colored cans next to a bin of soapy water on a table. The soap bubbles were so thick that I couldn't see what was inside.

"Let's go!" one of the lunch ladies said to me. "You have a long line behind you!"

It was a mistake to be first. I bit my lip hard to keep tears from starting.

"Food in blue," Jack chanted behind me. "Trash in black. Recycling in gray. Silverware in the soap."

"Thank you." I put my silverware in first, and then realized I had nothing to use to scrape the extra pudding off my tray. I had to take my spoon out of the soapy water and use it. Why hadn't I asked Jack to go first? When my hands were finally empty, I had soap bubbles on my fingers and my heart was pounding. I wiped my hands on my jeans and sat back at my seat, waiting for someone to tell me I could leave.

I didn't belong here. Maybe it had been a mistake to come. I'd never felt this unhappy in homeschool, even without Owen.

"School ends at two-forty," Jack said again.

I looked at the clock with him.

I can't wait.

Rabbits are the third-most surrendered pets to animal shelters, behind dogs and cats.

When I got off the bus, Dad, Mom, and Owen were sitting in the rocking chairs on the porch. As I walked down the driveway Mom held up her phone to take my photo, but I didn't have any smiles left in me. So I pretended I didn't see her and looked at Dad's truck in front of the barn. Last night when I went with him on his call, I had such high hopes for today.

"Welcome home!" Dad said, grinning.

I dropped my backpack onto the front steps and burst into tears.

Rocking chairs squeaked and then I felt Mom's arms around me. "What happened?" she asked softly.

I was embarrassed to be crying, but it felt so good to be hugged and to bury my face in her shirt. My answer came out in pieces. "Ev-er-y-thing."

"Come on, Em," Dad said, picking up my backpack. "Let's get you something to eat and you can tell us. Owen and I've been eyeing that blueberry pie all day, but we waited for you to have a slice with us."

The pie did make me feel a little better. At least I wasn't hungry on top of everything else. And being home, where I didn't have to try so hard, was a relief. I felt the day melting off me like dirt in a hot shower.

"It was so hard to make friends. At recess I just sat and watched other kids play kickball because I didn't have anyone to hang out with," I said, between mouthfuls. "My apple rolled across the cafeteria. And the lunch lady yelled at me. Then, when it was time to go home, I couldn't remember which bus was mine. I had to ask Shonna from homeschool group to help me figure it out. And she is only in third grade!"

"I'm sorry you had a hard day," Mom said. "How were the classes?"

I shrugged. "Okay. But I just got going with one thing and then it was time for something else. Math was easy and social studies will start off as a repeat. But I didn't finish the page of science questions, even though everyone else did. I spent too long thinking about the questions. I have to do a group project with some kids, too. We have to introduce each other to the class using the game Two Truths and a Lie."

"Well, there's a chance to make a friend, right?" Mom said. She sounded hopeful, like I had felt this morning.

I sighed. "I tried, but I don't think I can do this. I thought I was ready, but it's harder and less fun than I thought it would be. Maybe public school just isn't for me."

"You have to give it a chance," Mom replied. "It's only been a day."

Wait. What? That wasn't what I thought she'd say. "But when I said I wanted to go, you said it my *choice*," I said. "Remember? You even seemed a little disappointed that I wanted to go."

"That's because I knew I'd miss you," Mom said. "But you can't choose to give up when something gets hard, Emma. Everything has hard parts, especially when it's new. So we can talk about it after you get through those first hard parts."

"But how long will *that* take?" I asked.

"I don't know," Mom said. "Certainly more than a day."

Owen nodded. I looked away from him. I wanted him on my side.

That's when I saw the pet carrier beside the door—a rotten cherry on an already-terrible-day sundae. In the relief of being home, I'd forgotten.

We were taking Lapi to the shelter.

....

Carrying Lapi, I followed Dad across the parking lot to the Rangeley Animal Shelter. In the race, both Excited and Scared had sat down on the sidelines now. Sad was the only one running.

Lapi had put his paws up on the side of the pen when I went to get him, so happy that I was home. Holding him had made the whole day better, but then I had to put him in the carrier.

The shelter's lobby was bright with orange puffy chairs. There were colorful displays of leashes and collars, pet beds, and bags of food for sale. Soft music was playing, but a few dogs were barking somewhere beyond the doors.

Behind the counter, a woman smiled. "Good afternoon. Can I help you?"

"My daughter and I rescued a stray rabbit last night," Dad said.

As I lifted Lapi out of the carrier, the woman smiled. "What an adorable bunny! It's not easy to tell exact age with rabbits, but he doesn't look very old. Maybe a year or two. Let me check the lost-pet database and see if any-one has reported a gold-colored bunny missing."

As she typed on her computer, I stroked Lapi. I wanted my hands to remember everything about him—the size of his paws, the roundness of his back, and how his ears felt like soft flower petals.

I had wanted to believe that Pépère had sent Lapi to me with some rabbit magic for my first day of school. But today hadn't turned out anything like I'd hoped. And now, even Lapi was leaving me.

There was a hamster in a cage along the wall. Behind the cage was a window that looked into another room with more small-animal cages. Inside one was a white rabbit. His cage didn't look big enough for him to jump or twist or run very far.

"None of the lost bunnies match yours," the woman said. "So what would you like to do? Do you want to sur-render him to us?"

The word *surrender* did it. Lapi twitched as my tear hit his nose.

"Oh, Emma," Dad said gently. "It's all right."

I hate when adults say it's all right when you're sad. Some things just *aren't* all right. "He won't be able to hop around in those little cages."

"The rabbits get playtime outside their cage every day," I heard the woman say. "We'll take good care of him, I promise."

"Hear that, Emma?" Dad said. "He'll get playtime."

"Can't we keep him? Please?" I was begging, but I didn't care. "You and Mom won't have to do anything. I'll feed him and clean up after him and play with him each afternoon and every weekend so he won't be lonely." I talked super fast so Dad didn't have time to say no. "It would make school lots better, because I'd have something to look forward to at the end of the day. Please? Please?"

The woman and I both waited for Dad to say something. But he just rubbed his chin, thinking.

Finally the woman said softly, "Did you give him a name?"

"Monsieur Lapin," I said quietly. "But I nicknamed him Lapi."

I knew with each passing second, Dad's answer was more likely to be no. I kissed the back of Lapi's neck and concentrated on his smell: warm and rabbity.

He doesn't know what's coming. When we walk away, will he think I didn't like him? Or he did something wrong?

Surrender is a terrible word.

"His name comes from stories my father used to tell," Dad said. "He was a farmer up in Quebec."

I glanced over and saw tears in Dad's eyes, too. "But this rabbit simply doesn't belong to us, Em."

And right then I realized a funny thing about surrendering. Sometimes when you finally give up trying to make your first idea work out, you think of a second one.

I looked over at the woman. "Could Lapi stay with us *until* someone claimed him? And if no one ever did, could we keep him?"

She looked at Dad. "I do check the lost-pet listings every day. I could call you if his family reports him missing. Usually, though, if someone has lost a beloved pet, they report it right away. And from what I can see of his fur and nails, he's been on his own for a while."

Dad took a long breath.

The woman gave Lapi a sad smile. "The truth is that sometimes people get tired of taking care of pet rabbits and just let them go. They think they'll be able to survive in the wild and that's not true." She turned to me. "Rabbits can live up to twelve years, though. It's a real commitment."

"I promise that I'll take care of him every day," I said. "And if no one ever claims him, I'll still take care of him, even when I'm older and in high school. And if he can't come to college with me, I'll take online courses!"

Dad cracked a smile. "You don't need to do *that*. But here's what I'm worried about, Em. It's harder to give up something the longer you've had it. If someone does claim him, you'll have to return him. Are you sure you want to take that risk?"

I nodded.

"He's completely your responsibility," Dad added.

I nodded harder.

"Mom is gonna kill me," he muttered.

As Dad gave the woman our phone number, Lapi nuzzled against my neck. I laid my cheek on his ears. Even if I hadn't made a *kid* best friend yet, I had a rabbit one.

My knees felt like collapsing from having something finally go right today. Maybe Excited had just needed a break, because suddenly she was back in the race, even if she was way behind and limping.

Lapi was mine, at least for now.

Some rabbit pairs bond easily and others take a long time to become friends.

That night, I put **Be Yourself** and **You Got This!** back on the windowsill with the rest of my rock collection. I felt I'd failed at both of them. I didn't "get" school at all, and it didn't even feel possible to **Be Yourself**.

For tomorrow, I needed something easier. Maybe **Keep Going**? That rock came from the top of Mount Katahdin. Dad, Owen, and I climbed that mountain one day, and it was a hard hike at the top. I wanted to give up and sit by the trailside and wait for them to come back down. But Owen said, "Keep going," and I did.

Keep Going felt like work, though. Don't quit—even if you want to.

I wondered how long Mom would make me go to public school before I could change my mind and go back to homeschooling.

Lapi hopped over to a sweatshirt I'd left on the floor and dug at it until it was bunched up like a nest, then he flopped in it. It felt warm and safe to have Lapi here, like I didn't have to face all these hard things by myself.

Mom had said not to get attached to him, but I'd been carrying a hole inside me since Owen went off to school last year and this little rabbit had jumped right into that hole and made himself at home.

I smiled at Lapi chewing the tag off my sweatshirt. Maybe Pépère really *had* sent me some rabbit magic. Tomorrow if I got scared or sad, I could just think of him waiting for me, like my own little furry happy ending.

I imagined the people at school as characters in Pépère's stories. Ms. Hutton would be a beaver, always working hard. Ms. Martel would be a hummingbird flittering around the classroom. Iris might be a skunk, friendly but not always. Leah seemed like a pretty deer.

And Jack? He was a hard one. Maybe a bobcat hunting by himself. Or a red squirrel chattering about things he liked.

Somehow, imagining them as animals made things easier. I tossed **Keep Going** on my bed next to my backpack for tomorrow and settled down to do my homework.

In my assignment notebook, our group project was first on my list of things to do. I still felt annoyed that I hadn't had much chance to contribute to my group's ideas, but Iris had a point. A video would be easier on the day we presented, because the other kids would be watching the screen, not us. Also we could film more than one take if we messed up.

I tapped my pencil on my assignment notebook. We'd probably have to shoot the video outside of class, though. When would we do that?

I smiled as an idea formed in my mind. What if I invited my group over to my house? Even if we introduced each other in pairs on the video, there was no reason we couldn't film it together.

We'd get the project done and the other kids would be in my world instead of me trying to fit into theirs. I could ask Mom to get us some good snacks and they could meet Lapi! Now that Lapi was mine, I could tell the other kids about him. We'd have such a great time that it'd bounce us right over the friendship bump.

It was a perfect plan!

When I came downstairs to ask Mom about the snacks, Owen was talking to her in the kitchen. "If I make the soccer team, Jordan said I could ride home with him. I'll text you, but if I don't come home on the bus, it's good news."

"Okay," Mom said. "Fingers crossed! I'll be anxious to hear all about it."

"Mom, I'm going to invite my group-project kids over," I said. "Can you buy some good snacks?"

"Sure!" she said. "What day are they coming?"

"I hope *tomorrow*."

I was so excited to invite Iris, Leah, and Jack to my house. We'd have fun and they'd fall in love with Lapi, just like I did. After all, who wouldn't want to spend time with a cute rabbit?

He'd be my furry secret weapon!

When a rabbit stretches toward you with its ears tipped forward, it's curious and wants to share what you're doing.

I was determined to make the second day of school better than the first.

To help me **Keep Going**, I made a list in my assignment notebook of all the things that would be easier on the second day. By the time I got off the bus, I already had four things written down.

Easier the Second Day

1. I know where my room and desk are.
2. I know some of the kids' names.
3. I brought a bag lunch.
4. I have a plan to invite my group to my house.

I was so excited about the last one that I didn't even wait until Leah, Iris, and Jack had unpacked their backpacks. "So I was thinking about our project."

"Two Truths and a Lie!" Jack said.

"School hasn't started yet," Iris said.

Leah nodded. "I'm not even awake. I stayed up too late watching baby goat videos! My sister showed me one, and then we just kept clicking on more!"

"That sounds cute," I said, but inside I felt deflated, like when I'm excited to go on a hike and wake up to find it pouring rain outside. *Don't worry*, I told myself. There will be a right time to talk about the project.

To help me learn kids' names, I kept another list in

the back of my assignment notebook and put a star next to any potential best friends. I loaned a pencil to a boy named Matt and sat next to Sarah on the rug for morning meeting. Brandon liked to talk in class, which meant Ms. Hutton said his name a lot. So I knew six names out of the twenty-two kids in my class:

Leah *

Iris *

Jack

Matt

Sarah *

Brandon

I didn't want to have extra homework when my group came over. So as the morning went on, I tried to finish everything. Whenever Ms. Martel wanted Jack to move on to the next thing, she made a little circle spinning motion in the air with her index finger. If I caught my mind wandering, I'd secretly do that motion under my desk with my finger.

Move on. Keep going.

When lunch came, I still hadn't had the chance to ask Iris, Leah, and Jack over. But at least I had a plan for the cafeteria. I hoped the bag lunch would help me find a seat faster.

The chairs were already filling up when I walked into the cafeteria. I saw Iris and Leah's group had no extra seat for me. Sarah wasn't at any table yet. Matt had one seat open at his table, and even though the table was mostly boys, I figured he owed me for loaning him the pencil.

"Hi," I said, putting my bag lunch down at the seat next to him. I held my breath, in case he told me it was taken.

"Hey," he replied. "Thanks for the pencil."

I smiled. "No problem."

"Time for lunch," I heard behind me.

I turned around. "Oh, hey, Jack. Today I'm sitting here. Okay?"

"Yes." He didn't seem upset, but as he walked away, I felt bad. Jack had been nice to sit with me yesterday.

"If you had to choose one, would you rather never take a shower again or never brush your teeth?" a boy across the table asked Matt.

"I could just go swimming instead of taking a shower," Matt replied. "So I'd keep my toothbrush. Would *you* rather have smelly feet or smelly breath?"

"Smelly feet!" the boy said.

It wasn't much of a conversation, but it was one. I was trying to decide what I'd pick when the first boy said, "Hey, did you have time to watch that video I sent you about the bugs that live in your pillow?"

"Yes!" Matt said. "It was disgusting. It reminded me of last year. Remember when Mr. Patten——?"

The other boy laughed and slapped the table. "I know exactly what you're going to say!"

Around me, kids were talking and laughing. I never knew you could be surrounded by so many kids and still feel alone. I tried to stay focused on the boys at my table, but out of the corner of my eye I could see Leah and Iris were making funny faces at each other and laughing. Sarah was sharing her French fries with another girl. Jack was talking to Dustin and another boy at the back table.

When I got back to the classroom, I crossed out *I brought a bag lunch* on my "Easier on the Second Day" list. Today's lunch was just a different kind of hard.

In the afternoon, Ms. Hutton took us to the school library and told us we were allowed to choose any two books to take home. Going to the library was always one of my favorite things to do, and this library was so bright and beautiful. I couldn't believe it was all for kids! Tissue-paper tropical fish hung from the skylights and there was a big terrarium with a real live lizard in it. There were tables with chairs and bean bags and even some big balls to sit on at the banks of computers. And so many rows of bookshelves. I took a deep breath of that wonderful book smell, trying to hold in my excitement.

"After you choose your books," Ms. Hutton said, "you can spend the rest of the period reading or working on your Two Truths and a Lie presentations."

Finally! Now it would be the right time to invite the other kids over to my house. "I'll save us some seats," I said to Leah, Iris, and Jack.

I figured I'd be done choosing books first, because I knew what kind of books I wanted and where to find them. I'd spent a lot of time at our small public library and recognized the Dewey decimal numbers on the nonfiction shelves. I headed for the 630s. This time I wasn't learning about pet rabbits for a homeschool report, though. Lapi was depending on me, and I wanted to do everything right so Lapi would always love me best. Not like Maggie and Molly, who liked me fine until they had a choice. Then they always picked Mom.

I found two good books on rabbit care and took them to the desk to sign them out. On my way, I passed Jack. "Hey, after you get your books, meet me at one of the tables by the window," I said. "I have a plan."

He pulled out *The Encyclopedia of Animals* from the stacks without even looking at me. "Yes."

I picked a table with four seats and put extra books on

the empty chairs to save them for Jack, Iris, and Leah. It felt nice to be the person saving seats for a change.

I opened the first rabbit book and began reading the chapter "Understanding Your Rabbit." I had read and taken notes on the whole section before Jack sat next to me.

At another table, I could hear Brandon talking in a fake a British accent. Matt and another kid were smiling and laughing at him.

Jack opened *The Encyclopedia of Animals* and showed me the table of contents. "Chapter Twelve is Lagomorpha: rabbits, hares, and pikas."

"I've never heard of a pika," I said. "I'll have to look that up."

Jack flipped the pages. I hadn't meant *now*, but when he swung the book around to show me, the animal was adorable! Like a guinea pig with mouse ears.

"Wow!" I said. "That's so cute!"

"A pika barks when it's scared," Jack said. "Its nickname is 'rock rabbit.'"

"It doesn't really look like a rabbit," I said. "More like a—"

"You wascally wock wabbit!" Jack said in an Elmer Fudd voice.

The other kids stopped talking. They glanced sideways, frowning. How come when they talked differently, it was funny, but when Jack did it wasn't?

I guess when you already belong, it's easier to be different. "That's funny!" I said loudly, like we were joking and the other kids were wrong if they didn't think so.

"Pikas collect vegetation to store underground for the winter," Jack said. "They don't hibernate."

The other kids were definitely paying attention to us now. I could feel my face getting red, but talking to Jack was like sledding down a steep hill. Once the momentum kicked in, I'd be lucky if I could steer.

"They live in the mountains and need cool temperatures. As temperatures rise, they have to climb higher. With climate change—"

"Hi, I saved you a seat!" I waved to Iris and Leah.

I knew it was rude to interrupt Jack, but he wasn't stopping on his own and that was rude, too. Maybe Owen's advice to **Be Yourself** was really too simple. Maybe there was a point where being completely yourself stopped being a good thing and just became a lonely thing.

I moved the extra books off the chairs and waited impatiently while Iris and Leah sat down. "So I had a great idea about our project," I said. "We can meet at my house this afternoon after school and do the video. We wouldn't be rushed in case we need to do a few takes."

Leah gave me an apologetic smile. "I'm not sure I can get a ride. My mom and dad are at work."

"You can take the bus with me," I said. "It stops right at the end of our driveway. I'm sure my mom could bring you home after."

"You can't just take someone else's bus," Iris said.

Leah nodded. "You have to bring a permission slip from home and give it to the bus office first thing in the morning."

"Oh." The smile slid off my face. I didn't know that. "My mom could probably pick you up and bring you home," I offered.

"It's too complicated. Let's just work in twos," Iris said. "Me and Leah, you and Jack."

"But it'll look like two things, instead of a group project," I said.

"Don't worry, Emma," Leah said. "This is just a little project, not a big deal. It won't even count much toward our grades."

Not a big deal? But I wanted them to come to my house. I wanted them to get to know me at home, where it'd be easier to become friends. I wanted to do a good job on the project. I wanted a few things to go my way instead of changing all my ideas.

And saying "I want you to meet my pet rabbit" would just sound pathetic.

I could tell that Leah and Iris were getting frustrated with me, though. "Okay," I said quietly.

Ms. Hutton clapped her hands to get our attention. "We have about five minutes before we need to go back to the classroom. So come sign out your books if you haven't done so already."

"Can you come?" I asked Jack quietly.

He took out his phone. "It's just for emergencies."

I didn't know if the person he was texting would consider this an actual *emergency*, but within minutes we had a plan. Jack's mom would bring him to my house today after school.

Easier the Second Day

1. I know where my room and desk are.

2. I know ~~some~~ more of the kids' names.

3. ~~I brought a bag lunch.~~ Not actually easier, though I did use the right trash cans.

4. ~~I have a plan to invite my group to my house.~~ Only Jack is coming.

Rabbits have scent glands under their chins. They rub their chins on things to claim them as their own.

When I got home, Mom told me that Owen had texted. He made the soccer team.

Now he'd probably have practice every day. "That's great," I said flatly, unpacking my backpack. I could smell that she'd been baking something yummy. "What smells so good?"

Mom grinned. "I baked chocolate-chip cookies! How many kids are coming over today?"

"Only Jack," I said. "Thanks so much for making cookies, though. And can I borrow your phone? I'll need to take a video."

Mom nodded. "Sure. It's on the counter."

I put her phone in my pocket. "Um, just so you know," I said, feeling like I should warn her, "Jack's a bit different. I think he might have some special needs."

"Different makes life more interesting," Mom said.

I nodded, though that seemed like one of those easy things people say to gloss over hard parts. "He especially likes to talk about animals."

"Just like you," Mom said.

"Even more than me," I said. "In fact, if there were a TV game show where all the categories were animals, Jack could be a millionaire."

But when Jack and his mom arrived, I was surprised that he stepped back as Molly and Maggie came over barking, tails wagging.

"Girls," Mom said sharply to the dogs. "Go lie down."

As Molly and Maggie trudged to their beds, Jack's mom said softly, "It's a sensory thing. Jack loves to read about animals, but in real life they can be overwhelming."

"No problem at all," Mom said. "Can I make you a cup of tea or coffee while the kids do their homework?"

"Tea would be lovely."

"I'll put the kettle on," Mom said. "Make yourselves at home. And if you'd like to wash your hands, the bathroom is through that door."

"But no frogs are in there," Jack said sadly.

Mom laughed. "Oh, Emma told you about those? You're right. We don't have frogs in the bathroom regularly. That was just a homeschool science project. The frogs grew up and we let them go back in the pond where we'd found the eggs."

"Um. Let's work in my room, Jack!" I said quickly to change the subject. "My rabbit is there, but he only makes quiet sounds."

I got a piece of kale and a few blueberries from the

refrigerator for Lapi and the plate of chocolate-chip cookies for Jack and me. "Come on."

As we were climbing the stairs, I heard Jack's mom talking to mine in the kitchen. "Thank you for having us over. The other kids at school are mostly kind to Jack, but they almost never think to include him outside of school. So this is really nice."

"It's nice for Emma, too!" Mom said. "She's been hoping for a friend."

I felt bad that Jack and I were both getting left out of things. Being left out hurts. I turned to him and rolled my eyes, in case he was as embarrassed as I was that our mothers were talking about us.

But his eyes were focused on my bedroom door, his fingers flickering at his sides. He looked a little scared.

"It's okay," I said. "Lapi can stay in his pen, if you want."

When I opened my bedroom door, Lapi immediately put his paws up on the side of the pen, excited to get out and have a run.

"Later," I promised him. "Jack and I have work to do."

Lapi thumped his back foot on the floor.

"Rabbits thump to warn other rabbits about danger," Jack said.

"Usually," I said. "But *this* rabbit is telling me that he wants to have a run and he's mad that I said no."

Jack stared at Lapi, his fingers twitching harder. "Let me out of here!"

Did he mean Lapi? Or himself? "Are you okay?" I asked.

"I'm fine," Jack said plainly without taking his eyes off Lapi. "How are you?"

I smiled. "I'm fine, too."

Lapi thumped his back foot again. "He's mad that you said no," Jack said, his eyes bright with excitement. "He wants to come out!"

Was Jack asking me to let Lapi out? "Hey, I have an idea, but it's okay if you don't want to."

"A good idea?" Jack asked.

"Well, *you* get to decide if it's good or not," I said. "You could sit at my desk and pull your feet up on the chair. I promise Lapi won't jump up there. He can have a little run around the room, and then I'll put a treat in his pen and he'll go back in to get it."

Jack didn't look 100 percent sure, but he sat on my desk chair and put his heels up on the seat.

As soon as I opened the pen door, Lapi hopped easily onto my braided rug. His first free hops were always light and dainty: little front feet, big back feet. Then he'd pick up speed, darting under my bed and out again, with long leaps that were so fast, he'd lose his footing and slide on the hardwood floor.

Jack gave a high-pitched laugh. "He's a wascally wabbit!" he said in his Elmer Fudd voice.

"He sure is!" I said.

In between hops, Lapi would suddenly stop and rub his chin on something, claiming it. Dresser edge—MINE.

Heater—MINE.

Quilt—MINE.

Bookshelf—MINE.

Lapi paused and rubbed his chin on my foot, his whiskers tickling around my flip-flop. You—MINE.

"He's claiming me," I said.

Then Lapi suddenly leaped and twisted, like all the happiness inside him had exploded and lifted him into the air. He landed facing Jack.

"That's called a binky. I read about it in the rabbit book I got at the library. It means he's happy." I handed Jack a blueberry. "The book also said blueberries are one of their favorite things."

Jack threw the blueberry at Lapi's feet. He sniffed it and then ate it up.

"I should've known he'd love them," I said. "My pépère used to tell a story about how Monsieur Lapin tricked Monsieur Renard the fox out of his blueberries."

"What story?" Jack asked.

I hesitated. It was one thing to remember Pépère's stories or to tell them in our family. It was a whole different thing to tell another kid I didn't even know that well.

But Jack stared at me, waiting.

So I took a deep breath. "It happened once that Monsieur Lapin saw Monsieur Renard the fox sitting in a blueberry patch, grooming his beautiful red tail before he feasted on all those delicious berries."

"Foxes are omnivores," Jack said. "They eat both plants and animals."

"That's good to know," I said. "But Monsieur Lapin has magic and this is a story. So don't expect things to stay completely real, okay?"

"It's a lie," Jack said matter-of-factly.

"No." Though I guess if there were only two choices, it wasn't true. I shrugged. "Stories are somewhere in between. Do you want to hear it anyway?"

Jack nodded. "Yes."

As Lapi chinned the leg of the desk chair, Jack pulled in his feet tighter, his arms wrapped around his legs.

"Okay. So Monsieur Lapin said, 'Oh, Monsieur Renard, your tail is so glorious, but you've missed a spot.'

"Monsieur Renard was very proud of his tail. 'Where?' he demanded."

"What kind of spot?" Jack said.

"Um, pine pitch."

Jack nodded and I continued, "Monsieur Lapin pointed. 'Right there! No, a little more to the right. Almost! A little more to the right.' Soon Monsieur Renard was turning around and around, spinning so fast trying to reach the spot that he fell down dizzy. Monsieur Lapin jumped right into those blueberries and ate them all. So it was."

I couldn't tell the story as well as Pépère, but still, it had been fun to share it.

Lapi went up on his hind legs to look at Jack. Jack let his arms go. His fingers twitched hard as he slid one foot tentatively toward the edge of the desk chair.

I held my breath as Lapi moved his chin across the toe of Jack's shoe. Then he landed his front feet back on the floor and took off again, under my dresser.

Jack looked over at me, his mouth open.

"He claimed you," I said.

Jack kept his feet up on my desk chair, but his hands stopped twitching. "Let's touch him."

"You want to touch Lapi?" I asked, surprised.

"Only his back."

"Okay, but he doesn't like to be picked up," I said. "So sit on the floor and I'll put a blueberry next to you."

As soon as Lapi came over for the blueberry, Jack reached out one trembling hand—three quick, barely there touches. I waited for Lapi to hop away, but he didn't.

"He likes you," I said. "Maybe because your name sounds like a rabbit, too. Jackrabbit."

"Jackrabbits are really hares." Jack reached out and patted Lapi again, so lightly that I couldn't tell if he actually touched Lapi's body or just the very tips of his fur.

"Monsieur Lapin," he whispered. "And Jack Rabbit."

Rabbits don't consider breed, age, or size when choosing a friend to bond with.

I would've liked to hang out with Jack and Lapi all afternoon, but I imagined Ms. Martel with her spinning finger. We had to get our video done.

So I put the rest of the blueberries in Lapi's pen so he'd go in to get them. "Let's film our video before we run out of time," I said, closing the pen door behind him.

"I'll introduce you and you can introduce me. Did you bring any props to show when we reveal your answers?"

Jack opened his backpack and took out a plastic bag of Legos, *Dr. Seuss's ABC*, and some loose tickets like you'd get for a raffle or to attend an event.

"I learned to read at age three," Jack said. "'BIG A, little a—'"

"Great!" I said quickly before he launched into the whole book. "That's one truth. What about the Legos?"

"I like Legos."

Having grown up with Jack, the other kids would probably already know he liked Legos. "What's the coolest or best thing you've ever made with Legos?" I asked.

"A dinosaur skeleton."

"Seriously? How big was it?"

Jack held his hands wide apart.

"Wow! That's amazing!" I said. "Do you know how many Legos it took to build it? It doesn't have to be the exact number. Close is good enough."

Jack looked off into space. "Seven hundred and thirty."

I considered that. "Okay. That's a cool truth, but

maybe we should be extra tricky. What if we twist it to make that the *lie?* I could say, 'Jack once built a dinosaur skeleton with two hundred Legos.' Then for the reveal, we can say, 'Wrong! It was over seven hundred Legos!'"

Jack smiled. "Yes."

"What are the tickets for?"

He picked up one and read the back. "Raffle. Pumpkin Festival, Damariscotta, Maine."

"Did you win?" I asked. It was the only reason I would've kept a raffle ticket, to remind myself how good it felt to win.

"No." Jack picked up another ticket. "Raffle. Christmas Fair, First Parish Church, Rangeley, Maine."

"Did you win that one?"

"No. If you win, you have to give the ticket up," he replied.

"Have you *ever* won?" I asked.

"No."

I felt like I was bungling this. But maybe just because I didn't understand why he kept those tickets didn't mean there wasn't a good reason to Jack. And maybe I didn't have to understand why. Maybe just the fact he liked them was all that mattered.

"All right. That can be your second truth. You have a collection of raffle tickets." If we didn't get filming, we'd run out of time. "I want to change my statements from the ones I said at school. My first truth will be that I love to go kayaking. I used to go with my brother a lot, but now he's in high school and busier." I didn't really mean to tell Jack that. It just came out. "You'll just say 'Emma likes to go kayaking,' though."

I had a secret plan with that statement. I was hoping that some other girl would tell me that she liked to go kayaking, too. Then I could invite her over and we could go together and she could use Owen's kayak.

Jack ripped several sheets of paper out of his notebook.

"What are you doing?" I asked.

"Cue cards," he replied.

"Great idea!" I waited for him to write my first statement. "The second truth is I once climbed Mount Katahdin."

Jack wrote it easily, even spelling Katahdin correctly. I thought Ms. Hutton would like to know that we both like hiking and mountain climbing. I wouldn't tell her that I almost didn't make it to the top and Owen had to coax me to **Keep Going**, though.

"And the third one is 'Emma has a pet parakeet.'"

Jack paused, his pencil above the paper.

"It's the *lie*," I reminded him. "After the kids guess, I can show a photo of my real pets. A photo isn't as cute as the real thing, but—"

Wait.

What if I brought Lapi himself? Was that crazy?

On the one hand, that would be a bit complicated and a lot to coordinate. And I didn't even know if Mom would have time. Or if it was allowed.

On the other hand, it could be quick. If Mom could bring him, I could take him out of the carrier and let the kids pat him for a couple minutes. Then Mom could take him back home. It wouldn't take a lot longer than showing a photo.

But maybe Mom would start talking and tell the

kids something embarrassing about me, like how she told Jack's mom I wanted a friend.

Even if it was the truth.

Maybe Dad could bring him? Dad was a big part of Lapi's story, and he didn't tell embarrassing stories about me, thinking they were cute.

Suddenly I was glad Iris and Leah hadn't been able to meet Lapi yet—this would be even better! It could be a big dramatic moment for my reveal. Most kids love pets. Everyone would want to meet Lapi and talk to me about him.

Maybe it'd even bring me my best friend.

"You know how our program has three parts?" I asked Jack. "First, we say the statements about each other. Then the class guesses. Finally we reveal the answers?"

"Yes," Jack said.

"Okay, I have an idea. Let's do the statements about each other on video, just like we planned. I'll introduce you and you introduce me. But then on the day we present, let's do our own reveals *in person*! It'll be more exciting for the audience. You can bring your Lego dinosaur skeleton, or if it's too fragile to bring, maybe you could bring a big a photo of it? I bet kids would think it was awesome. It'll give you a chance to tell them about it. And maybe I can bring Lapi."

Jack smiled. "Yes!"

It felt great that Jack was excited about my idea! It made me feel a little braver about telling Iris and Leah that Jack and I had changed the plans.

"Okay, let's get filming. I'll go first," I said. Since one of Jack's truths was about reading, I stood in front of my bookcase. "Just film me no matter what happens. We can edit later."

I don't like being recorded and wished I had made some cue cards, too. But I smiled my friendliest smile as Jack pushed the button on Mom's phone. "Let me introduce you to Jack! Here are some statements about him, but only two of them are true. See if you can guess the lie." I paused for extra drama. "Jack collects raffle tickets. Jack built a dinosaur skeleton with two hundred Legos.

Jack learned to read at the age of three." As I said each statement, I tried to keep my face the same so I wouldn't give away the lie. "Which one do you think is the lie?"

Then Jack stood in front of my dresser. I arranged the cue cards on the windowsill behind me so the lie would be last. I wanted to end with Lapi.

"Let me introduce you to my friend Emma!" Jack said loudly, like he was an announcer at a basketball game. "Emma likes to go kayaking! Emma once climbed Mount Katahdin! Emma has a pet—parakeet! Which one is the lie?"

Listening to Jack say things about me in such a big way felt weird. Like hearing about someone else, even though I did like to kayak and climb mountains.

But so what? The other kids didn't seem to be taking this assignment so seriously. And I had to start somewhere. The only way the other kids would ever get to know me was if I shared things about myself.

It might work out perfectly, too. I imagined one of the girls in my class hearing Jack talk about me and then seeing Lapi. *Wow!* she'd think. *Emma is so interesting!*

She'd ask if she could pat Lapi. I'd say, "Sure!" and then we'd talk. I was pretty confident that I could take it from there on my own. It was just so hard to get started.

Even though this felt weird and uncomfortable, it would all be worth it if I found a best friend.

A bonded pair of rabbits that spends too much time apart will unbond.

"And the varsity team is almost all juniors and seniors, so it's unbelievable that I made it," Owen said that night at supper. "Coach says I won't start, but that's okay. Just being on the team will be enough."

Enough to make you busy every afternoon. I swirled a piece of spaghetti on my plate with my fork.

"Yes, that's amazing!" Mom smiled at me. "And Emma had a friend over today."

"Hey, that's great!" Owen said.

The happy way he said it annoyed me, like now all my problems were over. And I knew he knew better. "Jack was the only one who could come," I said flatly. "When you're done, can you take a photo of me kayaking with your phone? I need it for school."

"Do we actually have to go out on the water? Could you just be sitting in your kayak?" Owen asked. "I have some homework."

"No. That would look ridiculous." No one would want to go kayaking with me on the grass! I looked down at my plate. "Please? We don't have to go far."

"Okay." As soon he finished supper, Owen got the paddles and I got the life jackets. When you're the warden's kids, you always have to follow the rules. It's not that I ever *wanted* to get into trouble, but I knew there'd be extra disappointment if I did.

Looking out across the lake, I saw we had it almost to

ourselves, with just one canoe gliding along the far shore. Most of the summer people had already gone home, closing up their camps and pulling their docks out of the water. It was so quiet that I could hear a woodpecker drumming on a tree across the lake.

I threw my flip-flops into the bottom of the kayak. Holding my paddle across the front, I climbed in.

"Take my phone while I push you off," Owen said.

I tucked his phone into my pocket. I love that moment when Owen gives me a shove out past the drop-off and suddenly it's just water under my kayak. I think it must be close to what a bird feels when it lifts off and flies. A quick burst, and then you leave the ground behind you. It's a free feeling, with nothing holding you back.

"Where do you want to take the photo?" Owen asked, paddling up beside me.

"I want Eagle Island behind me." On maps, it has a different name, but Owen and I named it for the big eagle's nest in a tall pine tree at the tip. When the eagles were nesting or had eaglets, we weren't allowed on the island, but the juveniles had flown off weeks ago. We still saw them in the treetops around the lake from time to time, but they were on their own now.

Kayaking to Eagle Island would take a little time, too. Time that I didn't have to share Owen with anyone.

The lake was almost flat, just a breeze wrinkling the surface. As I paddled, I cut a path through the ripples. A little kingfisher cackled at us, flying low over the waves. He landed on a dead branch that stretched over the water. As we caught up to him, he flew off again, complaining.

Owen was digging his paddle so hard that my arms were getting sore trying to keep up with him. The breeze kept blowing my hair across my nose, and it itched every time. Finally I gave up and let him get ahead.

I took his phone from my pocket and shot a photo of him kayaking away from me.

Approaching the island, I looked at the empty nest, a big mess of sticks waiting for next year. When the eagles nested again in late winter, the lake would probably still be a huge field of ice.

It's hard to imagine winter in other seasons, but it's a different world out here. Light reflects on the ice, and the wind blows strong because there's nothing on the lake to slow it down. It roars against my bedroom windows and whispers through the tiny spaces around the back door. The wind also sweeps the ice clean, so clear and smooth that ice skates fly over it.

Owen and I barely went skating at all last year. I missed shouting and hearing our voices echo out in the middle. I missed how Mom would put the outside light on to tell us when it was time to come back. If we were skating way out in the middle, the light was small, a tiny dot of yellow in the darkening air.

Maybe Owen and I'd go skating this winter. Soccer would be over by then. Or maybe he'd sign up for something else at school that he'd do without me.

But at least now I had Lapi at home to keep me from feeling lonely. If things didn't get better at school, I wondered how long Mom would make me wait before I could go back to homeschooling. Surely before winter came.

I didn't like to quit anything, but sometimes things just don't work out and it's better to admit it and try something else. I imagined Ms. Martel spinning her finger: "Move on."

"Okay, give me my phone," Owen said. "Then paddle ahead so the island will be in the background."

As he shot photos, I smiled, trying to look fun and outdoorsy.

"I'll email those to you," Owen said. I thought he'd start for home, but he kayaked past me to the island.

As I beached my kayak next to his, Owen picked up a small rock and threw it. "Beat that."

I picked up a rock and threw it as hard as I could. It didn't go as far as his, so I tried again.

We threw rocks over and over, watching the ripples speeding outward and connecting with each other. I threw with my whole arm each time, but I still couldn't beat his.

"We should head home," Owen said finally.

I reached down and picked up one last stone. I slipped it into my pocket.

"What will you write on it?" he asked.

"Hope," I said.

"I can't believe you don't already have that one," Owen said, picking up another rock.

"I've always had hope. I didn't need a rock to give me extra." I sighed. "Do you ever wish you could go backward?"

"Not usually," Owen said. "But that doesn't mean I don't miss some things."

I couldn't look at him. I wondered if I was one of those things, but I was too afraid of the answer.

"If I could go back," I said, "I'd go back to a day when you and I were at Pépère and Mémère's house. I miss those days a lot."

Owen nodded. "Me, too. I don't think I'd want to go backward for good, though. I'd miss some 'now' things."

"But you wouldn't know about the 'now' things because they wouldn't have happened yet," I said.

Owen looked at me. "Is school really going so terribly that you want to go backward?"

I lifted one shoulder. "Well, no one has bullied me or

pushed me into a locker, or any of the other mean things kids do to each other on TV shows. Mostly kids just ignore me." I looked down at my feet. "It's harder to be different than I thought it would be, though. You'd think with all those kids, it'd be easy to make friends, but it isn't. It seems like most kids already have enough friends, and they aren't looking for any more."

"It might look that way," Owen said. "But everyone wants friends. Remember that, okay?"

"Okay," I said, though it didn't seem true. "I do have a plan that might help. I'm going to ask Dad if he'll bring Lapi to school as part of my group project. I bet the kids will like him and I'll be the girl with the adorable rabbit, not just the new kid with red hair."

Owen smiled. "I hope Lapi brings some rabbit magic with him, like Pépère used to say."

He remembered.

I nodded. "Me, too."

"Pépère would have a story about Monsieur Lapin going to school," Owen said. "Monsieur Lapin would sneak into the cafeteria and raid the salad bar. The lunch ladies would go to serve lunch and find the lettuce bin empty."

I laughed. "And no carrots or blueberries!"

"I'm glad Dad let you keep Lapi," Owen said. "Though I knew the second I saw him that if the shelter didn't know where he belonged, he'd be coming back home with us." He grinned. "It's hard to say no to you when you really want something, Em. Dad didn't stand a chance."

I grinned back. "That's because Lapi belongs with us."

Owen picked up his paddle. "We should get back now, though. It's getting dark and I really do have homework. Did you want me to push you off?"

"Okay."

Paddling toward home, the sun was setting, reflecting in our upstairs windows. I aimed the bow of my kayak at the beach in front of our house and beat Owen home.

That night before I went to bed, I found Owen's rock on my pillow.

Rabbit Magic.

Bonding rabbits isn't always a smooth process. Sometimes a few steps forward is followed by a step backward.

First thing the next day, I told Leah and Iris my idea. They had shot down my other ideas, but this time, I had Jack on my side. "Jack and I filmed our statements about each other, but we decided to do our own reveals *in person*. It'll be more interesting for the audience."

"I don't like to talk in front of the class," Iris said, unpacking her backpack.

I put my hands on my hips, ready to argue.

But Leah said, "I like Emma's idea. She's right, that'll be more interesting, and if we're holding something for the reveals, it's not as hard as just standing there."

Iris shook her head. "Let's just—"

"Take a vote!" Jack said.

The vote was three to one to do the reveals in person.

Iris didn't look happy, but I didn't worry about it too much. We had done everything her way up until then. "Jack and I changed some of our statements, too."

"The frogs were a homeschool experiment," Jack added.

My smile froze. "Um, I was homeschooled," I blurted out, hoping Leah and Iris didn't hear exactly what he'd said. "My new truths are that I climbed Mount Katahdin and I like kayaking."

"With Owen," Jack said. "Though he's busy now."

"Homeschooled? Do you mean you've *never* been to school?" Iris asked.

The words weren't mean, but the way she said it sounded like I didn't know anything.

"I did my schoolwork at home," I started to say, but

I was relieved to see Ms. Martel coming over just then. "Jack came to my house yesterday," I told her quickly, to put distance between me and the homeschool subject. "He met my rabbit."

"I touched him," Jack said. "Only on his back."

Ms. Martel's eyebrows went up. "You did, Jack? That's great! How did the rabbit feel?"

"Happy," Jack replied.

Ms. Martel opened her mouth like maybe she was expecting him to say "soft," but then she smiled. "And how did *you* feel?"

"Scared," Jack said.

"And you touched him anyway?" Ms. Martel asked. "Good for you, Jack."

"I think it's cool that you were homeschooled," Leah said to me.

She does? I smiled. "Thanks!"

"Do you want to sit with us at lunch today?" Leah asked. "Nora has book club, so there's an empty spot at our table."

Jack looked at me. "You won't get away this time,

Monsieur Lapin!" he said in his Elmer Fudd voice. "You wascally—"

Please stop talking, Jack. It makes you stand out and not in a good way. "Sure! I'd like that," I said loudly.

I was in over my head. Jack and I had fun when it was just us, but it was harder to be his friend in a group. While homeschooling, I mostly saw friends one or two at a time, so I could always adapt and meet them in the middle between us. Here, that middle seemed to be constantly changing and sometimes disappeared altogether. And I'd never tried to be friends with kids who weren't friends with each other before.

Leah rolled her eyes sympathetically at me.

Right there I knew I had to choose. I liked Jack and I wanted to be friends with him. But I really wanted to be friends with some girls, too. And this was my first real chance.

I rolled my eyes, too.

Rabbits are territorial. Be careful and respectful when reaching into a rabbit's space or you may be charged at or even bitten.

For the first time since school started, I was excited for lunch. I had a place to go, a seat waiting for me at a table with other fifth grade girls.

It'd only be for today since I was just a substitute for Nora. But maybe I could be a regular on Nora's book club day.

When I reached the table, all the chairs were full

except one with a spiral notebook that said "Elise" across the top.

As Elise moved the book for me, I felt like I was floating inside.

"Hi!" I grinned and sat down.

They all looked nice. Everyone said their names, but I was concentrating so hard on looking friendly that when they were done, I didn't remember a single one, except Leah, Iris, and Elise.

"Emma has never been to school before," Iris said. "She was homeschooled."

I sighed. Did that have to be the *first* thing the other girls knew about me?

"So what do you think of public school?" a black-haired girl asked.

"Parts of it are fun," I said. "But it's too long."

They all laughed. "You can say that again!" the black-haired girl said. "I'm ready for another vacation!"

I gave her a real smile. It felt good that I had made them laugh, even if it had been by accident.

"I'd hate being homeschooled," the girl with the pigtails said. "I'd be so bored being at home all day with nothing to do."

I opened my mouth to say I hadn't been bored, but everyone else was nodding. When they got to know me better, it'd be easier to tell them the truth. For now, it seemed more important to fit in. "I wanted to give public school a try and see if I liked it."

"You should join chorus!" the girl with the pigtails said. "That's super fun! We even go to a concert in Boston every year!"

I grinned. That *did* sound like fun.

"Do you play sports?" Elise asked.

I nodded. "But I haven't had many chances to be on a team. I really like—"

"Time for lunch," I heard behind me.

Uh-oh. I thought Jack understood I was having lunch with Leah's group today.

"Hey, Jack," I said. "I'm sitting here today. Okay?"

"Yes," he said.

As soon as he was too far away to hear, Leah said, "I'm sorry you got Jack as a partner for our presentation. He can be hard to talk to."

I couldn't tell if she was saying it to be mean or just stating a fact. "Unless it's about animals," I agreed, unwrapping my sandwich.

That wasn't mean. It was just the truth, right?

"He's why Ms. Martel comes to our room," Leah explained. "She acts like she's there to help out with everyone, but really, she's Jack's aide. When he was little, he used to throw tantrums. Remember?" She raised her eyebrows to the other girls.

"Wild tantrums!" Elise agreed. "And be careful what you tell him. He doesn't always get that some things are private."

Iris groaned. "Remember last year, Akari?"

The black-haired girl rolled her eyes. "He told Mrs. Keller about the surprise party we were throwing for her, even though we told him not to!"

Elise. Akari. I willed myself to remember the names until I could write them down in the back of my assignment notebook.

138

"She caught us making some decorations," Akari said. "She asked what they were for. And he just told her the truth!"

"I'm glad he's not in my class this year," Elise said.

I tried to concentrate on my sandwich, but I was squirming inside. It didn't feel good talking about Jack, even if everything they said sounded true.

I felt lucky the other girls didn't know the mistakes I'd made when I was younger, too. Like the time I locked my whole family out of our house and it was snowing. We had to wait in the barn until a locksmith came. Or the time I accidentally ate some dog biscuits because they were in a plain plastic bag and looked like crackers.

Friends can tease you over dumb things like that and it's funny. But if you're not friends, it hurts.

Maybe if these girls knew those things about me and a bunch more, they wouldn't want to be my friends, either.

I wished I hadn't rolled my eyes about Jack with Leah.

Leah took a bite of her sandwich. "Ugh! I told Mom to

ask for no pickles! I don't know why she can't remember that I don't like them." She smiled at me.

Oh no! I fought to keep smiling as Leah plucked pickles out of her sandwich and put them on her napkin. "You can have them, Emma."

I wanted to say "Thanks," because it was a friendly thing that she was sharing something with me, but— "That's okay. Really."

"It's no problem," she said. "I don't like them."

Six pickle slices. "Oh, yum," I said, trying to sound excited as she slid the napkin to me. "Would anyone else like some? I don't want to hog them."

"I don't like pickles," Iris said.

"No thanks," Akari said.

Leah was still smiling at me, so I took a nibble off the edge of the first pickle. I wanted to make a horrible face, but I forced myself to nod. "Mmm." I took another tiny bite and moved the pickle piece way over to one side of my mouth, away from my tongue.

"I think my family is going to the movies on Saturday," Iris said. "If we do go, do you want to come, Leah?"

Leah sighed. "I wish! But we're going to New Hampshire to see my grandparents. It's so boring. It's a really long ride and then we just sit in their living room and talk. Or actually mostly I listen to *the adults* talk. I just nod and say 'uh-huh' every now and then."

The girls all laughed, but it was still hard for me to talk about grandparents. Especially with kids who still had theirs.

"So does anyone have pets?" I asked.

"I have a gray tiger cat," said Akari.

The girl with the pigtails laughed. "Tell Emma his name!"

"I named him when I was little, Martha!" Akari protested, laughing.

Elise. Akari. Martha. "What is it?" I took a bite of my sandwich to take the pickle taste away.

Akari shrugged. "Ketchup."

The other girls were laughing, so it seemed okay to laugh, too. "That's funny," I said.

Martha had a cat named Jake, and Iris didn't have any pets. "My dad is allergic," she said.

"I have a dog named Bear," Leah said. "He's a black lab, but he thinks he's a lapdog!"

Leah had been nice to give me her pickles and she even had a dog! Nice + pet lover = perfect best friend possibility.

"I have two dogs named Molly and Maggie," I said, excited to finally find something fun that we both liked to talk about. "And we just got a rabbit named Lapi."

"Wow! I love rabbits!" Leah said. "I've always wanted one, but my parents think Bear would scare a rabbit."

"Lapi actually bosses our dogs around," I said, grinning. "When he gets racing and hopping, it freaks them out."

"La Pee sounds like he has to go to the bathroom," Iris said. "If you got another rabbit you could call him La Poop."

The girls all laughed. I smiled, like I found it funny, too. The name was special to me, though, and definitely not a joke. "It's a family name," I said, and then to change the subject, I added, "My dad and I found him."

"What do you mean you found him?" Akari asked.

I took another tiny nibble of pickle. I was hoping my

tongue would get numb to the taste, but it was just as awful as the first bite.

"He was a stray," I explained. "My dad's a game warden and he got a call saying a rabbit was stuck in a lady's fence. I went with him, and when we got there, it was a pet bunny, not a wild one."

"I would love to rescue animals!" Akari said. "How did you know the bunny was a pet?"

"We only have New England cottontails and snowshoe hares in Maine," I explained. "I knew just by looking that he wasn't either of those. Lapi is honey colored with a brown nose."

This was going really well! I felt like I had finally broken through the friendship wall and was making progress.

"You're lucky he wasn't a girl!" Akari said. "My friend got a pet rabbit and it had babies! So they had six rabbits instead of one!"

I nodded, though it did sound like fun to have baby bunnies at our house. "My dad checked. He's definitely a boy."

"Bunnies are cute, but they don't do much," Martha said. "They just sit and stare at you."

I didn't think that at all. Of course, Lapi wasn't like Molly and Maggie. They liked to play and would sit on the couch with us. "Lapi is a quiet kind of fun. But I love to watch him pull down his ears with his paws to groom them. And it's so cute when he flops onto his side or races around the room."

And he liked me. I could tell every time he chinned me or rose up on his hind legs to see what I was doing or if I'd brought him a treat.

"I'd like to meet Lapi," Leah said. "Maybe I could come over sometime?"

I was already planning to bring Lapi to school, but having Leah over to my house would be great, too! "Sure! And if you needed a ride, my mom could pick you up and bring you home." *Wait. Did that sound desperate?* "I mean, if you wanted to."

"That would be fun," Leah said. "Maybe my mom could call yours?"

"I'll give you our phone number!" We hadn't made

specific plans, but *almost*! I popped the rest of the pickle in my mouth.

"Our new neighbors lost a rabbit over the summer," Iris announced. "I saw posters for it."

The pickle was so sour that I wanted to gag. I chewed fast to get rid of it.

"There was even a reward of fifty dollars!" Iris added.

I stopped chewing. *Wait. What?*

"Did you try to find out who your bunny belonged to, Emma?" Martha tilted her head sympathetically. "Maybe it's the same one."

The same bunny? I swallowed the pickle as fast as I could. "We took Lapi to the shelter and the lady there checked on the computer about lost pets," I said. "No one had reported him missing and she promised she'd call if someone did."

"I didn't see any posters," Leah said to Iris. "Where were they?"

"On a few telephone poles," Iris said. "You weren't home much this summer."

"That's true," Leah said. "I went to see my cousins in Oregon, and then I went to camp."

"I'm sorry, Emma. But maybe you could get the reward?" Martha said.

"It's not him," I replied firmly. It just *couldn't* be. "The lady at the shelter said it looked like he'd been on his own a while. She said sometimes people let pet bunnies go thinking they'll survive in the wild, even though they won't. I'm sure that's what happened."

"Are the posters still up?" Akari asked Iris.

Iris shook her head. "It *was* a while ago that I saw them. My mom told me the family's last name is Abbott, though. They moved into the big house at the end of Morton Street."

"The shelter lady said people call right away when they want their pets back." I fought to keep the mildly interested look on my face, but inside my heart was speeding.

"Iris said they're new. Maybe they didn't *know* there's a shelter," Akari said.

"Iris, maybe you and I could walk over to their house and ask them?" Leah suggested.

"No! Let *me* check with them," I said quickly. "I bet my brother can find out their phone number for me. Or my dad could get it for me. That way, um, they can ask me questions."

I didn't want to call, but I needed time to think. I took a pen and wrote on my napkin.

Iris looked over at the words I'd written: Abbott. Morton Street.

"Yup," she said. "That's it."

I couldn't help thinking her words were truer than I wanted them to be.

Yup.

That's it.

To offer grooming, hold your hand on the ground in front of the rabbit. If the rabbit accepts, he will come to you.

Scared had been training in secret. She was miles ahead with Excited nowhere in sight.

More than anything, I wished school were over and I could go to my room, close the door with Lapi, and never come out. It was so unfair. Lapi could've died if Dad and I hadn't rescued him. And he loved *me* now.

The girls kept talking as they ate their lunch, but I hid the rest of the pickles in the napkin. I didn't even care about pretending I liked them anymore.

How could this have happened? I'd pushed the worry that Lapi might belong to someone else far into the background. And the idea of coming home from school without Lapi there made me want to cry.

Maybe the Abbotts hadn't loved him very much. Maybe they'd been so mean to him that he ran away.

And even if they *had* loved him, Iris said the posters were down. So they must've given up on finding him. Maybe they had a new rabbit by now.

When lunch was finally over, I told Leah I'd catch up to them at recess and went into the girls' bathroom near my classroom to pull myself together. There were other girls' rooms in the school, but I just wanted something familiar even if it was a longer walk.

I'd hoped to have the bathroom to myself, but there was another girl washing her hands. I picked a sink close to the door and didn't look at her.

I didn't know what to do. I'd only agreed to give Lapi back if the shelter called. I never agreed to go *looking* for his owner.

But a small, whiny, know-it-all voice inside me whispered, "But it's not *right* to keep him if he doesn't belong to you."

"Time for recess."

In the mirror, I saw Jack in the doorway, waiting for me. All I wanted was a moment to myself to figure out what to do. But there was nowhere to be by yourself at school—not even in the bathroom!

"Not now!" I snapped. "Can't you see I'm in the girls' room?"

Hurt jumped into Jack's eyes. At once, I knew I'd made a mistake. I hadn't meant to yell. It just came out that way. As he turned and ran, all my worries exploded out of me. "Wait!"

In the hallway, I saw Jack disappear into our classroom. We weren't supposed to be in there at recess, but I didn't care. Even if I got in trouble, nothing could be worse than how I felt already.

When I stepped inside, the classroom looked empty. *Jack wouldn't climb out a window, would he?* Then I saw his sneaker toe sticking out from under the big long table in front of "Ms. Hutton's Fabulous Fifth Graders" bulletin board.

I crawled under the table with him. Jack's face was buried in his arms across his knees.

"I'm so sorry," I said. "I just needed to be alone for a minute."

Jack didn't lift his head.

We sat in silence, just the sound of the clock ticking and the muffled voices of kids going outside. All morning I'd wished the clock would go faster, but now I didn't want those hands to move at all. In fact, I wished I could go back to the night before school started. Before I realized how hard it was all going to be. Back when Lapi was just mine. And anything seemed possible.

But I guess "anything" includes bad things, too.

"Something horrible happened at lunch," I said quietly. "But no matter how awful I feel, it wasn't right that I took it out on you."

"It wasn't right," Jack echoed into his arms.

I felt ashamed that I had yelled at him and hurt his feelings. Jack had sat with me when I didn't have anyone. He'd voted for my idea against Iris. I'd told him things I hadn't told anyone else, including one of Pépère's stories.

And I'd rolled my eyes and yelled at him. So what if Jack wasn't exactly like everyone else? I wasn't, either.

If Pépère were here, I knew what story he'd tell me. It'd always been one of my favorites, but I understood it in a new way today.

"Can I tell you a story?" I asked. "It's about the day Monsieur Lapin tried to be like Madame Sittelle, the nuthatch."

"Why?" Jack asked into his arms. "A nuthatch is a bird."

I wasn't sure if the "why" part went with "Can I tell you a story?" or with Monsieur Lapin wanting to be a nuthatch, but I answered the last one. "Because nuthatches can climb up and down tree trunks and peck out tasty bugs."

Jack lifted his head. "Rabbits are herbivores."

I nodded. "True, but Monsieur Lapin has rabbit magic, remember? Anything is possible."

"Yes," Jack said slowly, not sounding completely convinced.

I kept going anyway. "So it happened once that Monsieur Lapin decided that he'd climb a tree and get some tasty bugs to show off to Madame Sittelle that he could do anything she could."

"Nuthatches can go down a tree trunk headfirst," Jack said. "Only a few birds can do that."

"Really? That's another reason for Monsieur Lapin to be jealous!" I replied. "So he tried to climb the tree, but rabbit claws aren't made for climbing bark and he got scared halfway up. And when he tried to climb down *headfirst*, he fell to the ground."

I'd added that in just for Jack.

"Did he get a concussion?" Jack asked.

"No, he was only embarrassed, not hurt," I said. "And then Madame Sittelle said, 'Silly Monsieur Lapin. You'll never be a nuthatch. You are a rabbit.' Then she flew up into the trees and climbed down the tree trunk headfirst with food to share with him. They ate it together as friends. So it was." I looked at Jack. "That's one of my favorite stories. I think it means that a real friend will like you for you. And even if you aren't exactly alike about everything, that's okay." I gave a small shrug. "It gives you something to need from each other. Sometimes I have to be—"

"Emma Nuthatch," Jack said.

I smiled the first real smile since lunch. That wasn't what I was planning to say, but it worked.

"And you are Jack Rabbit," I replied.

....

We stayed under the table so long that my legs ached and I heard the kids coming in from recess. I couldn't move, though. Not yet. I felt safe under there and when I crawled out, that safe feeling would be over.

I'd have to deal with the napkin in my pocket.

"The horrible thing that happened at lunch was about

Lapi," I said quietly. "Someone lost a rabbit, and maybe it's him."

Jack stared at me. "Maybe it's him?"

I nodded, tears filling my eyes. "I'm scared to find out if Lapi belongs to that other family. I have to call them and I don't know what to say."

Jack crawled out from under the table. *Where was he going? Didn't he hear what I said?*

Now I was all alone.

Then I heard Jack ripping pages from his notebook. "What are you doing?" I asked, coming out from under the table.

"Cue cards," he replied.

Jack handed me a pencil. As I wrote, my hand shook so hard it didn't even look like my handwriting.

Hello. My name is Emma and I found a rabbit.

**A rabbit will grieve the
loss of a mate.**

That night after supper, I went to Owen's room. "Can
you help me with something? I need to find out someone's phone number, and they haven't lived here very
long."

He looked up from his homework. "Can't you just ask
them?"

I shook my head. *Please don't ask me any more questions.*

"Okay. Well, if they have a landline, we can probably look it up online."

For once, I was glad for the miserable cell phone service in the mountains. Most people still had landlines at home because they were more predictable.

As Owen opened his laptop, I pulled the napkin out of my pocket. "All I have is a last name and the street they live on." I tried to act normal, though my insides were exploding into sharp pieces. "They moved here over the summer."

Owen looked at the napkin. "What's this about, Em?"

I swallowed hard. "Um, it's just that something came up at school. I need to ask someone a question."

It was pretty clear that I wasn't telling him everything. But telling the truth isn't always as simple as in Two Truths and a Lie. Sometimes the whole truth is just too much to say at once.

"I might even be able to find out a first name for you," Owen said. "No guarantees, though."

"That's okay," I said quickly. "If you get me the phone number, I'll take it from there."

While Owen searched online, I looked around me. His room had changed, but he still had a Lego boat we built together on his shelf. It made me happy to see it there, like maybe he still cared about it.

I wished I had thought to show it to Jack. He probably would have liked it, even if it wasn't as impressive as his dinosaur skeleton. Maybe I could invite him over again? But if I did, what would that mean? Working on an assignment together was one thing, but hanging out was another, and school seemed to have a lot of social rules that I didn't know.

Owen wrote a phone number at the bottom of the napkin. "Try this one, Em. If it's not right, come back and I'll keep looking."

"Thanks." I started to go, but I paused in the doorway. "Owen?"

He looked up from his textbook.

"Why do you keep that old Lego boat?" I blurted out the question fast, before I could change my mind.

"The Lego boat?" He looked up at his shelf. "I don't know. I just like it. We worked hard on it. And I like to remember us putting it together. It was fun, remember?"

I nodded. "You aren't afraid your friends would make fun of you if they saw it?"

He shrugged. "A little teasing would be okay. But a real friend would see that it mattered to me."

I sighed. "That kind of friend is hard to find."

"Yes, and you have to be that kind of friend back," Owen said. "It works both ways. So you also have to *be* the friend you want to have."

I opened my mouth to say, "I have been!" but then I sucked my bottom lip. Had I *really*?

Owen grinned. "Hey, Em. This might sound silly, but let's make another big Lego project together after soccer's done and things aren't so busy."

"I'd like that."

Part of me doubted it would ever happen. After

soccer there would probably be something else. But even so, knowing that he wanted to do something with me filled that empty space inside me.

I wished I could tell him the real reason for the phone number. But if I told him, I would have to call.

And I wasn't ready.

Back in my room, I told myself it was too late. Maybe the family had little kids who were in bed.

I'd have more time on the weekend.

I should practice my reveals first. I needed to get my props together.

But deep inside, I knew timing wasn't the problem. Every time I looked at Lapi hopping around my feet, chinning everything in sight, I didn't want to call.

I'd rescued Lapi, but now I needed him to rescue me. I needed him to be there when I got home from school. I needed him to love me best. And I needed to believe that Pépère had sent him to me to bring me rabbit magic.

Or maybe that was just wishing.

Maybe there was no rabbit magic. Maybe Lapi was

just someone else's stray pet and I was just a weird girl that no one wanted for her best friend.

I put the slip of paper with the name and address with the cue cards at the very back of my assignment notebook.

And then I closed it tight.

Rabbits have a blind spot in front of their nose. It's the only place they can't see.

Let me introduce you to my friend Emma! Emma likes to go kayaking! Emma once climbed Mount Katahdin! Emma has a pet—parakeet!

In my room, watching Jack describe me on the video, even my truths didn't feel completely like me. But as Leah had said, this was just a little project and I didn't have to make this such a big deal.

I'd start with the props. I opened the email Owen had sent with my kayaking photos. The first ones were exactly what I'd asked for: me with Eagle Island in the background. Then I came to the photo I'd taken of Owen. The nose of my kayak was in the foreground of the shot and Owen was far enough ahead that he was slightly out of focus.

I'd print that one, too. Just for me.

I had planned to ask Dad if he could bring Lapi to school as a surprise. But then Iris would see Lapi and ask if I'd called yet. And maybe if I talked about him, I'd cry.

I decided to bring a photo of Molly and Maggie, instead. I loved them, too. Maybe I could even find a good photo from last Halloween. I had dressed as Alice from *Alice's Adventures in Wonderland*, and Molly and Maggie had worn big bow ties and spinning caps as Tweedledee and Tweedledum. I bet the kids would find that funny.

For the last truth, I went to the windowsill for my Keep Going rock. I didn't have to show anyone what it said, but it was still from the mountain.

Outside the window, it was almost dark, but I could still see the trees and the mountain on the other side of the lake. I missed seeing the lake change during the day. Amazing all the things you don't even realize you'll miss until you leave them or they leave you.

Looking at **Keep Going** in my hand, I found myself thinking about Jack. He'd kept going, trying to be my friend, even as I was hoping for someone else.

Owen's words suddenly hit me hard, "You also have to *be* the friend you want to have."

I looked over at my checklist.

Emma's Best Friend Checklist
Likes me best.
Likes the things I like.
Shares secret jokes.
Is always on my side.

Lets me be me.

Forgives me when I'm sorry.

I hadn't lived up my checklist myself. Not with Jack or Owen or even Lapi.

I hadn't always been on Jack's side.

Owen had let me be me, but I only wanted Owen to be himself if it included me. I didn't want him to change and leave me behind.

I wanted to keep Lapi mine, because I needed him.

In fact, I'd wanted them *all* to be the kind of friend I needed, but I hadn't tried as hard to be the one they needed.

Maybe it was too much to expect one person to be my "everything" best friend anyway. Maybe I already had what I needed, just spread out across a bunch of people. Some parts with Owen. Some parts with Lapi. Some parts with Jack. Some parts with Leah, even. Some parts to come with kids I didn't know yet.

But I had to be a best friend, too.

I picked up the napkin. Lapi loved us now, but maybe he had loved his first family, too. With all my heart, I wanted him to stay with us. But what did *he* want?

I knew what I had to do. Even if it was hard or embarrassing or people got mad at me, I had to tell the truth about everything.

Even if it meant that I lost Lapi.

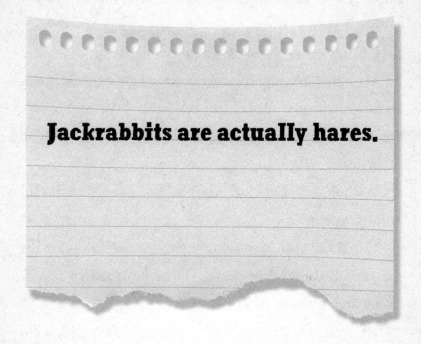

Jackrabbits are actually hares.

On presentation day, Scared was definitely running ahead of Excited.

Some of the other kids looked nervous, too, though. Maybe it wasn't just me. Maybe standing in front of everyone and sharing something important about yourself was just plain hard.

Last night when I decided to ask Dad to bring Lapi,

I'd only told him what time to come to surprise my class. But when he came into my classroom carrying the pet carrier, I got a surprise, too.

Owen stepped into my classroom with him.

Ms. Hutton's eyebrows went up when she saw them. Her eyes widened to see the pet carrier. "Welcome," Ms. Hutton said. "You must be Emma's family. Such a nice surprise!"

"I thought you cleared this with her," Dad said quietly to me.

"I told her you were bringing my reveal, but not what the reveal was," I whispered. Then I turned to Owen. "Why aren't you at school?"

He grinned. "I had study hall and then lunch, so I asked Dad to pick me up. I know you've had a rough week, and I remember how hard my first week was. I wanted to cheer you on."

Excited grabbed the back of Scared's shirt and yanked her backward.

Ms. Hutton smiled at me. "This looks like a fun ending to our program. We'll let you go last, Emma."

Last would be perfect! But as the other kids stood up and we guessed their lies and saw their reveals, I started to wish I could just do mine and get it over with.

I did find out some interesting things, though. Matt liked hiking, just like Ms. Hutton and me. Solange had twin brothers. Sarah collected sea glass. Brinn also had a pet rabbit! I couldn't wait to talk to her about it.

And some of the lies were funny. Matt said his dad was a secret agent. Jaden told us he had won a beauty pageant as a baby. Mikayla said she had a cousin who was a movie star.

I loved watching the "Ms. Hutton's Fabulous Fifth Graders" bulletin board fill up with photos of my classmates' special people, places, and pets. The table showed off cool objects: Sarah's sea glass collection, the glittery slime that Brinn had sold at a craft fair, and Kara's favorite stuffed animal moose.

Everyone had interesting things about them, and I was excited to ask some questions to get to know the other kids better. Even if we didn't become best friends, regular friends were good, too.

"Our last group is Iris, Leah, Jack, and Emma," Ms. Hutton said.

Leah and Iris went first. As their part of the video played, Jack's fingers were fluttering his secret wave at his sides.

My hands were shaking, too, rattling the photo in my hands. I hoped no one noticed, but even if they did, so what? Some other kids had seemed nervous, too.

When it was my turn to introduce Jack, it was weird to see myself on the classroom TV standing in my bedroom in front of my bookshelf. I wondered if Jack would notice that I had reshot the video last night and it wasn't the one he'd filmed.

"Let me introduce you to Jack. His nickname is Jack Rabbit. Though, as Jack will tell you, jackrabbits are not actually rabbits. They're hares."

"Capable of speeds up to forty miles an hour," Jack said under his breath next to me.

"Before coming to school here, I was homeschooled, and Jack has been a real friend to me. Here are some statements about him,

but only two of them are true. See if you can guess the lie. Jack
collects raffle tickets even though he has never won a raffle. Jack
built a dinosaur skeleton with two hundred Legos. Jack learned to
read at the age of three."

Most kids guessed the raffle statement was the lie.

"Wrong!" Jack said. "The dinosaur skeleton had seven hundred and thirty Legos! I brought a photo to show you because the real model could break!"

"Wow!" I heard kids gasp as he showed the photo. "That's amazing!"

Even Owen leaned forward to look, impressed.

After everyone had admired Jack's photo and seen his book and tickets, Ms. Hutton took the photo to put on the bulletin board. "Jack, is there anything else you'd like us to know about you?"

"No," he said matter-of-factly.

I raised my hand. "Could I give something to Jack?"

Ms. Hutton nodded. "Of course, Emma."

I reached into my pocket and pulled out a rock. "It's not a raffle, but you win this, Jack. I want you to have it."

He turned it over in his hand. "Rabbit Magic," he said, reading the words.

"My pépère used to say that all rabbits have magic. And you have Jack Rabbit magic of your own," I said. "Thanks for being my friend."

Jack smiled, handing me one of his tickets. "You give up the ticket when you win."

I smiled back and put the raffle ticket in my pocket.

"Thank you, Emma," Ms. Hutton said. "Jack, now it's your turn to tell us about Emma."

Jack started the video. *"Let me introduce you to my friend Emma! Emma likes to go kayaking! Emma once climbed Mount Katahdin! Emma has a pet—parakeet!"*

The kids guessed correctly that the parakeet was the lie. It was pretty easy since Jack had hesitated as he said it, but I didn't care.

"You're right." I said. "But actually, none of them are the whole truth."

Ms. Hutton looked up from the notes she was taking. I wanted to get a good grade on this and these photos would be on the bulletin board for a while. But I also wanted to take a chance and be my whole self, even if the other kids didn't understand or I got a bad grade.

"My brother, Owen, took a photo of me kayaking, but that's not the photo I brought for the bulletin board. I do like kayaking, but I've always liked it best with Owen. We don't go as often as we used to because he's in high school and busier now. But even though I miss him, I'm really proud of him. And it's extra special when I get to spend time with him." As I turned the photo around, I looked slowly at Owen to see if he was embarrassed. When I chose the photo of him, I didn't know he'd be there to see it.

Owen smiled at me. I saw nods from some of the other kids, too, like they understood. I felt lighter, almost dizzy with relief. I had said the truth and it had been okay. Better than okay—I felt understood.

"The second truth is that I did climb Mount Katahdin and this rock is from the trail." I held up the rock and turned it over to show the words. "My brother wrote 'Keep Going' on it, because I wanted to quit part of the way up. But you don't ever get past the hard parts if you quit."

I couldn't quit here, either. The hardest one was last.

"You're right that I don't have a pet parakeet," I said. "But we do have two dogs and, for a while, we've had a pet rabbit. My dad and I rescued him as a stray, and I named him Lapi for the stories my pépère used to tell about a rabbit named Monsieur Lapin. I asked my dad to bring Lapi so you could meet him." I gestured to Dad and to Lapi peeking out of his pet carrier.

"Yay!" Kara said. "A bunny!"

"He's adorable!" Brinn added.

"Can we pet him?" Leah asked.

I nodded. "But first I have to tell you the whole truth." I felt my throat filling with emotion. I pushed ahead anyway, hoping I could finish before the tears started. "I said he was our pet for a while, because I found out there were some signs up in town about a missing rabbit."

I heard a gasp from the other kids. Owen and Dad exchanged confused looks.

"My brother helped me get the family's phone number." My voice was really shaking now. "I need to call them. If Lapi belongs to them, I have to give him back."

Beside me, Jack reached into his pocket and took out his phone.

"Thanks," I whispered to him. "But I didn't mean *now*."

"It's just for emergencies," he said, still holding it out to me.

It did *feel* like an emergency, even if it wasn't the 9-1-1 kind. I looked at Ms. Hutton. "Could I call? It would be great to get this over with."

She nodded. "We're all worried *with* you. Do you want to practice first?"

"Actually, Jack helped me make cue cards. I think I'm ready." I got the phone number and cue cards from the back of my assignment notebook.

Dad came over beside me. "I'm sorry, Em."

"Me, too," I replied. "But I promised you I'd give him back if we found his family. And it's like the wild animals you bring home. Even if you wish you could keep them, they need to go back where they belong."

The other kids circled around me. I couldn't believe how concerned they all looked.

"Everyone, cross your fingers!" Matt said.

Seeing them all crossing their fingers, even Iris, gave me some extra courage.

Jack held the cue cards so I could read them. Owen put his arm around me as I called the number and pushed the button for speakerphone so everyone could hear.

Waiting, my eyes went to the bulletin board full of everyone's special photos. Ms. Hutton had already put up the photo of Owen and me kayaking. Seeing my photo surrounded by everyone else's made me smile. For the first time, I felt like maybe I could actually belong here.

"Hello?" a woman said.

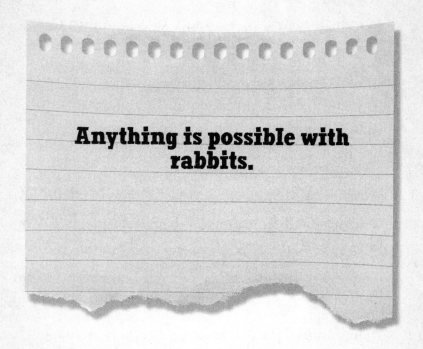

Anything is possible with rabbits.

Scared was the only one running.

"Hello. My name is Emma and I found a rabbit," I read off the cue card in Jack's hands. "I heard that you lost yours?"

"Yes!" the woman said happily. "Thank you so much for calling! The kids will be thrilled! We just moved here over the summer, and while we were unpacking, Clover got out of her pen. We'd given up hope!" She sounded nice, at least.

"My dad and I found a rabbit this summer," I read. "We—"

"Her!" Owen whispered hard in my ear.

Wait. What? Then my brain caught up with me.

"Did you say *her* pen?" I asked.

"Yes!" the woman replied.

A girl! What if she'd made a mistake, though? I couldn't let myself feel relieved—not yet. "The rabbit I found is a boy," I said carefully. "My dad checked, but he said it's sometimes hard to tell with rabbits. Are you *sure* yours is a girl?"

"I'm positive. She had babies when she was younger." The woman sounded very disappointed. "Are you sure *yours* is a boy?"

I looked at Dad.

He nodded. "Definitely."

Scared took a nose dive and hit the track hard. "Ours is a boy!" I said. "A little honey-colored bunny with a brown nose."

"Oh," she said sadly. "No. Clover is a white New Zealand. That's definitely not our rabbit. Thank you for calling, though."

"Wait! Don't hang up!" I said. "There's a white rabbit at the Rangeley Animal Shelter! I saw it when we brought our rabbit in to find out if someone was missing him. Maybe that white rabbit is Clover?"

"Really? Oh, maybe it is! I'll call them right away!"

"I hope you find her," I said.

"I hope your rabbit finds his home, too," she replied.

I grinned. Lapi *had* found his home. "Thank you."

Everyone was quiet as I hung up the phone. Then they all started talking at once.

"Hooray!" Brinn said.

"I thought I might throw up, I was so worried!" Brandon said.

"I'm so glad!" Leah added.

"We only have a few minutes before lunch, so let's make the most of it," Ms. Hutton said. "Everyone who wants to, come sit on the rug so we can meet Lapi more easily."

"And I have bits of parsley that you can give him," Dad said, passing it out to the kids. "It's one of his favorites."

Owen set Lapi's carrier on the rug. He had barely opened the door before Lapi poked his face out. Then he hopped onto the rug and binkied!

"Oh, he's so cute!" Sarah said.

As Lapi hopped around the rug and ate parsley, Iris came over to me. "I'm really sorry," she said quietly.

Sorry? "It's okay," I said. "It all turned out great."

She looked at the floor. "There was a photo of a white rabbit on the poster. I knew it wasn't Lapi."

My mouth dropped open. "You lied?"

"It wasn't really a lie," Iris said. "I just didn't tell you *everything.* You wanted to be Leah's friend and I've been her best friend forever. I didn't want you to squeeze me out."

I stared at her. Part of me wanted to yell at her. I'd worried so much and she knew all along that it wasn't Lapi!

But another part of me understood. I'd felt left out

about Owen having new friends, too. It's hard to be left behind by someone important to you.

"It's okay to have more than one friend," I said. "And for friends to change. I've been thinking about that, too."

She smiled. "Martha is absent today if you want to sit with us at lunch."

"Thanks." It was nice of her to offer, but I had other plans. "I'm asking Jack if I can sit with him."

"Lapi's out!" Brinn said.

I turned to see that he'd squeezed through the half-open door to the hallway.

"Don't worry! I'll get him." I smiled at Dad. "I'm a trained Rabbit Wrangler!"

But the long hallway was perfect for racing. Lapi looked at me with that flash of freedom in his eyes and took off, faster than I could run! He went into the first open door he found—the girls' bathroom.

Jack caught up to me. "You guard the doorway, okay?" I said. "Don't let him get out."

It wasn't easy to grab Lapi, even with no one else in

there. He hopped under the stalls and slid on the floor. He binkied between the sinks. I finally cornered him at the trash can.

Jack was standing in the doorway, his arms and legs out to block Lapi from escaping. "Silly Monsieur Lapin," he said. "You'll never be a nuthatch. You are a rabbit!"

I laughed. "You're right," I said, holding Lapi against my heart. "None of Monsieur Lapin's friends ever wanted him to be something else. They liked him already." I smiled at Jack. "So they ate together as friends—even though rabbits are herbivores."

Jack nodded. "Because it's magic."

So it was. The first week of school had been harder than I could've dreamed, but I could feel change coming, like when the wind suddenly shifts on the lake and you know the storm is passing. Rabbit magic had come, or maybe it had been there all along, and I just didn't see it. There were things I still missed about homeschooling, but now there were some things I'd miss about public school, too. Maybe that's just how growing up is, like Going Forward and Looking Back are in a race. You know Going Forward will win, but you can't help rooting for Looking Back sometimes, too.

"You are a wascally wabbit!" Jack said in his Elmer Fudd voice.

Walking to our classroom, I let joy and relief fill me. I was grateful that Lapi was still mine, but even more than that, I felt free. I had been my whole self, and it'd been okay. For the first time, I knew why Lapi had binkied as soon as we'd released him from the fence. Freedom is just too big to hold inside you.

Right there in the hallway, not caring who saw me, I held Lapi tight and jumped into the air and twisted.

A perfect Emma binky.

Author's Note

When I talk to readers, I'm often asked, "Where do your ideas come from?" My books always start from tiny seeds of real life. Then I water those seeds with my imagination until a story grows. Having some real things and feelings underneath the story makes it all feel more real, even if most of the story is made up.

For *Because of the Rabbit*, here are the real seeds that started Emma's story:

Growing up in my family, I was the youngest. I have always loved and looked up to my older sister. When we were very young, I wanted to do everything she did. But as we grew older, some things changed. She started doing more things with her friends, and I remember missing her when that happened. So I gave those left-behind feelings to Emma, who experiences them with her older brother, Owen.

My husband's parents spoke French and older generations of his family came from Quebec, Canada. My own two children had a mémère and pépère (pronounced in North America as: MEM-may and PEP-pay). My children's pépère died before they were born, but he was a storyteller who loved nature. One way we have kept his memory alive for my children was through retelling his stories.

My grandmother was a big part of my childhood and she gave me her love of animals. To this day, I remove spiders from my house by putting a glass over them and carrying them outside, because she said we should always protect living things that do us no harm.

I have an adult son with autism who also loves animals and information, as Jack does in *Because of the Rabbit*. My son has highly sensitive senses, and real animals can be too loud or smelly or act in ways that startle him. So sometimes it's easier for my son to love animals in books more than in person. Being different and thinking differently can be a big strength, though. My son has brought lots of wonderful new ideas and new people into our family.

I homeschooled my own children when they were young. We started because of my son's sensory sensitivities. A regular school building was painful for him. It was a difficult decision, but then we found that we all enjoyed homeschooling. My son was always homeschooled, at least part-time. My daughter was homeschooled from the end of third grade through middle school. She and I had many honest conversations for this book about the excitement and hard parts of starting public school after homeschooling.

Lastly, we have rabbits! Five years ago, I adopted two rabbits from an animal shelter. Their names are Blueberry and Muffin, and because of them, I fell in love with bunnies. Rabbits are soft and sweet, but they are also very smart and tricky! Now we have three pet bunnies, and we also foster rabbits for a rescue. Over the past two years, we have fostered twenty-six rabbits, including the six baby bunnies we have at our house right now!

So my books always start from a real seed or many real seeds planted together. If you want to try that in your own writing, think about:

- Places that have been important to you
- People you've known
- Pets you've had
- Things you've wondered about
- Times when you've felt powerful emotions (lonely, scared, excited, different, jealous, angry, or loved)
- Things you've done

Then water those real seeds with your imagination and see what grows!

About the Author

Cynthia Lord is the award-winning author of *Rules*, a Newbery Honor book and a Schneider Family Book Award winner, as well as the critically acclaimed *A Handful of Stars*, *Half a Chance*, and *Touch Blue*. She is also the author of the Shelter Pet Squad chapter book series and the Hot Rod Hamster picture books and readers. Lord is a former teacher, behavioral specialist, and bookseller. She lives in Maine with her family, a dog, and three pet rabbits. She and her family have also fostered over twenty-five rescue bunnies. Visit her at cynthialord.com.